THE KILLING SPREE

Ned Embrel and his roaming gang of raiders go on a killing spree in the quiet, unsuspecting town of Leeward. However, they make the mistake of calling at the Circle E ranch on their way out of the area. They drag Sam the wrangler to his death and leave the owner, Captain Tom Evans, badly wounded.

So, young John Gideon Shaw once more finds himself on a trail of retribution. For Embrel and his riders, the Mexican border town will prove to be no hiding place. This time the raiders chose to violate the wrong town, the wrong ranch and the wrong man.

THE KILLING SPREE

THE KILLING SPREE

by

Harold Lamb

Dales Large Print Books
Long Preston, North Yorkshire,
BD23 4ND, England.

British Library Cataloguing in Publication Data.

Lamb, Harold
    The killing spree.

      A catalogue record of this book is
      available from the British Library

      ISBN   1-84262-043-6 pbk

First published in Great Britain by Robert Hale Ltd., 1999

Copyright © Harold Lamb 1999

Cover illustration © Lopez by arrangement with
Norma Editorial

Published in Large Print 2000 by arrangement with
Robert Hale Ltd.

939929887

Dales Large Print is an imprint of Library Magna Books Ltd.

Printed and bound in Great Britain by
T.J. (International) Ltd., Cornwall, PL28 8RW

ONE

Ned Embrel grunted as he eased himself off the bed and stepped over to the table near the window. He splashed water from the pitcher into the bowl and, sluicing the sweat from his lean body, he mopped absent-mindedly with the sparse towel, as he looked at himself in the long mirror. A bearded man of average build with blue eyes set close to a long thin nose stared back. He leaned towards the mirror and gave his newly clipped beard closer inspection.

'Not bad. Not bad at all,' he muttered to himself. Two hours ago he had had a full heavy set that had run into his hairline. Embrel turned to grab his clothes from the chair and proceeded to dress himself.

'You did a good job on my beard,' he grunted over his shoulder to the woman

7

who lay watching his ablutions from the bed. 'What d'you say your name was?'

'Nell,' she replied softly.

He stepped back and took a final appraisal.

'Well, Nell, you certainly are an all round satisfying creature.'

The saloon whore lay still and relaxed, waiting for the man to either bolster his praise with a few extra coins or make an empty-handed promise for a future visit.

'If you like I'll keep my time free, while you're in town,' she said, smiling invitingly. Perhaps he would toss another few dollars on the bedside cupboard. She had pleased him; he had said so.

Their attention was suddenly diverted as shots rang out from the street below. Nell gasped and clutched the bedcover to her as more shots rang out below in the saloon.

'Stay still,' Ned Embrel muttered, as he grabbed his gunrig and stepped to the window. Buckling on his belt, he glanced quickly up and down the street before drawing his gun and turning to face the saloon girl. Nell's nervous smile faltered as her eyes went from the gun, which was now pointing at her, to the gunman's face and saw the evil look that had come into his eyes. The levelled gun was the last thing she saw or heard as it fired. The bullet hit her in the left eye, emerging from the back of her head to splatter blood and bone over the pillow and wall behind her.

Ned Embrel picked up the money he had given her earlier on and placed it in his pocket before leaving the room.

A shot went off in the room next to the one he had just vacated. He banged the door with his gun.

'Crawford, hurry it,' he bellowed.

The door opened and Crawford stood there grinning.

'Coming boss,' he said, buckling on his rig.

Embrel looked beyond him. On the bed was the bloodstained body of a nude woman. Embrel nodded. 'Come on, the fun's about to start.'

A door opened at the far end of the landing and a man's head peered out – a loosened tie hanging noose-style round his neck.

'What's going on there, mister?'

Embrel pointed his gun and fired. The man fell back inside the room. The door slammed shut and the lock could be heard snapping on.

The two men sprinted along the landing and Crawford tried to open it. The rattling produced a series of screams from behind the locked door.

'Just another whore,' Embrel said, side-stepping to the top of the stairs as Crawford drew his gun and fired repeatedly through the panels. The screams from behind the locked door were suddenly cut off.

Both men left the landing and hurried down the stairs to join and assist the two men who were holding guns on the saloon bartender as he emptied the cash till onto the bar. Embrel fired and wounded a would-be hero causing the rest of the clientele to shrink back further into the walls of the saloon. Scooping the money into a bag, the four raiders left the saloon, firing their guns into the air as they went as a further deterrent.

More muted gunfire echoed out from along the street as the bank and other establishments were raided. Pandemonium broke loose in the town as the gunmen emerged into the street, firing indiscriminately as they made their way from one establishment to another, looting and killing. People were caught in the crossfire as the townsfolk tried to defend themselves and their property. Some were killed, others were wounded running for cover, as the raiders banded together and made their way to the far end of the street where their horses were waiting with one of their gang members.

Like a pot of hell boiling over, dust rose and roiled along the street, masking the carnage, as ten horses and riders rode out of

Leeward. The raiders left many dead or injured people in their wake. Male or female, it had not mattered. As far as Ned Embrel and his gang were concerned, nobody who had seen them close up had been left alive to identify them.

The gang thundered away from the shattered town. Four miles out of Leeward they slowed and halted. Then, gaining the high ground, they waited and watched the trail they had just covered to see if a posse was in pursuit. Once satisfied that there was nobody hot on their heels, Ned Embrel and his men relaxed their vigilance.

'Did we get much?' somebody said.

'A few thousand, d'you reckon?'

Embrel nodded. 'Enough to last for a while.'

Raking his horse with his spurs, he joined the trail again and set off south. The rest of his gang picked up the pace and followed close behind him. The ground rolled steadily and more evenly beneath their horses' hooves as they entered the broad grasslands and soon they were travelling through an area the horizon of which was dotted with a herd of young cattle. Even from that distance, Embrel could see they were yearlings. He signalled to his men and the band of ten riders slowed down and made their approach to the nearest group. Embrel frowned quizzically, surprised that there was not even one accompanying herder, as they walked their horses among the grazing cattle and he noted the Circle E brand, prominent on their rears. The main ranch could not be far away. Picking up speed the riders set off across the grasslands, not lessening their pace until in the distance they made out a ranch and outbuildings. It looked big and prosperous.

Strange, Embrel thought as he looked about him. There was still no sign of any cowboys or older cattle. Raising his hand, he stopped his horse and turned to Crawford, who reined alongside him.

'Not many cattle for such a big ranch. No sign of any riders either.'

'You're right, boss,' Crawford agreed, glancing about him before turning in his saddle to look behind him nervously. 'What have we stopped for?' he asked, wanting to put a much greater distance between himself and the town of Leeward.

'Use your brain, Crawford. Big ranch, no cattle to speak of, no riders,' Embrel grated. 'They could be on a drive. Let's go and take a look. Could be more easy pickings.'

Embrel turned towards the spread and the group bunched up behind their leader. There was no sign of any ranch hands as they entered the ranch environs. Nearing the main buildings, they spaced themselves fanshape behind Embrel, pulling to a halt at his signal.

A Negro came out of the ranch house and stood on the porch. Embrel kneed his horse forward so he looked directly down on the man.

'We would like to water our horses,' he said, touching his hat in mock courtesy. The man stared up at Embrel and then past him to his men. He had a feeling of foreboding for he knew that it was not water they wanted: there was plenty of water in the area.

'What's going on out there, Sam?'

He turned as an elderly man came to the door, leaning heavily on a stick.

'We just want to water our animals,' Embrel said, straightening his back, his eyes taking in the surrounding buildings. 'This is quite a spread, old man.'

'His name's not old man. He is Captain Evans,' Sam said indignantly. 'And this is his place. You're on Circle E land.'

'It's OK, Sam,' the owner said, taking a few painful steps on to the porch. 'Let them have some water, then they can be on their way.'

Embrel thanked him but made no move to dismount. He waved his hand about. 'This must take some looking after.'

Captain Tom Evans, suddenly aware of impending danger but unable to move with alacrity because he was crippled with rheumatism, stood motionless, crouched over his stick.

'Where's your range crew?' Embrel asked.

It was Sam who answered. 'On a drive and they's due back any time.

Ned Embrel drew his gun. 'That's all we want to hear,' he said. 'Search the place. There must be something worth taking, here.'

Captain Tom Evans tried to get back into the house. Embrel watched his painful struggle to turn at speed, then, like a cat playing with a mouse, he waited till the old man had got one foot inside the room before he shot him down.

Sam made a dash from the porch. If he could reach it, he had a gun in the bunk-house.

The riders laughed as they gave him a head start before arguing as to which one of their group was going to 'Go get 'im'.

One of the gang, Wilson by name, loosed his lariat and rode in pursuit of his quarry. The rope spun out and the loop fell over

Sam's shoulders. Pulling it tight, Wilson accelerated and Sam was pulled off his feet and dragged, mercilessly, behind the horse.

Leaving one of their number with their horses, the rest of the gang turned their attention to looting the ranch house. Going from room to room, smashing up furniture as they went about their searching, they came upon a small amount of money. One of the men, named Grady, searched the fallen ranch owner, Tom Evans. Grady took the gold timepiece he found in the old man's waistcoat pocket and the few dollars that were in his trousers. Another of the gang took a new Winchester repeater and a bottle of liquor.

'That's it. Time to go,' shouted Embrel. 'Let's hit the trail.'

His men trooped out of the ranch house and across to their horses. The rider who had roped Sam still rode up and down with the unrecognizable bloodied bundle, bouncing behind him. One of the gang pulled a knife and sliced the rope. 'Come on, Wilson. I think you've killed him, you heartless bastard.'

The man called Wilson tossed the parted rope aside and rode off laughing like a hyena.'

Embrel and his men rode on south towards Mexico. Once there, he and his men would spend their ill-gotten gains on drink and *señoritas*. They would enjoy themselves till the money ran out. Then they would ride out again on another killing spree.

At the border, the ten riders would split up into three parties. Each would travel to a separate town. They would meet again in San Credo, one month from that day. This was a plan that had proved successful in the past and which was duly followed.

The money was counted and shared out equally.

The three parties of murderous raiders waved a cheery farewell to each other as they rode away. They had money to spend and their thoughts were on whiskey, women and gambling. Embrel, who had shot the rancher, rode away with Crawford and a man called Tom Hall.

Wilson, who had so cruelly dragged Sam to his death, rode with Keely, Nolan and Smith.

Grady, the man who had taken Tom Evans's watch, rode with Jansen and Boyd.

South of the border the silence of the night was sporadically broken by coarse language and the odd gunshot in harsh contrast to the eerie silence that pervaded the Circle E ranch and the town of Leeward.

TWO

Buck Beanpole banged two empty tin pots together. Pat Wilkes, the ramrod, opened his eyes and stretched himself awake, cursing the cook for making such a racket. The young man lying beside him, hauled the blanket over his head in an attempt to shut out the din. Buck leant over the recumbent form and banged the pots again before hooking his boot under the blanket and, with one quick upward movement of his foot, sent the blanket flying high.

'Come on, young fella, we'll be home today.'

The broad-shouldered form of John Gideon Shaw curled into a tighter ball as he tried to bury himself into the ground. 'Go away, Beanpole, it's still dark,' he mumbled sleepily.

'If you just open your eyes, you'll see daylight,' the cook retorted testily, with an encore of rattled pots for good measure.

The young man groaned and sat up. He knew the lanky cook would not let him sleep on. Neither he nor Wilkes nor the three other ranch crew, who were muttering their dissent at being roused so early. If Buck Beanpole was awake and ready to move on … so be it.

John Gideon yawned and reached out, his fingers searching for his gun-belt. Buck Beanpole let out a loud tut-tutting noise to register his disapproval. Shaw took no notice of the big cook. The young cowhand got to his feet and slinging the belt around his waist he buckled it before tying the gun by its cord around his thigh. John Gideon knew the lanky cook did not like him carrying the handgun but he still wore it. It was his way of feeling safe and secure.

Making his way to the campfire, he picked up a tin cup and, filling it, he sipped the hot, strong coffee, before letting out a long sigh to let Buck Beanpole know it was of its usual good standard.

Rubbing the sleep from their eyes, the rest of the crew came up to the fire to join Pat Wilkes and John Gideon as they sat eating their breakfast. The men knew what was expected of them. Breakfast over, they would break camp and make for the Circle E to arrive sometime in the afternoon.

Pat Wilkes allowed more time than usual for their banter as he glanced around the group of cowhands. They had worked well on the drive which, this time, had been relatively problem free. The cow loss had been small and there had been no trouble with rustlers or anyone else. The weather had been accommodating and the pasture good. The cattle had fetched a good price, the money order for the sale was safely folded in his pocket and they would soon be back at the ranch. The cattle drive had been successful and he reckoned Captain Evans would be pleased with the transaction.

His glance fell on John Gideon Shaw, who,

catching his eye, offered him a top up for his coffee mug.

'No, thanks, not for me, son,' the ramrod answered, making a move to break up the sojourn.

He smiled as he watched the young man rise and adjust the gun at his hip.

There's a young man who's grown in size and confidence, Wilkes thought, and rightly so. There was not much anyone could teach John Gideon Shaw about guns or anything else, come to that, he recalled. John Gideon was the fastest gun the ramrod had ever seen and a crack-shot with his Winchester repeater and his old Sharps .50, which were stored in Buck Beanpole's chuck wagon.

As well as being a top cowhand he was a good horse wrangler and well thought of by the captain and Sam, the chief wrangler.

As they broke camp, Buck Beanpole did his usual spell of yelling at the crew to hurry up.

John Gideon took no notice except to intercede on behalf of the others if he thought the cook was being too stroppy. The lanky cook treated him like a son and their banter was always friendly. Both men stood tall; Buck being the taller at six foot five inches while John Gideon was only six foot two. With the chuck wagon packed and the horses readied, Buck climbed aboard and they set off with Pat Wilkes and John Gideon riding ahead.

Later that day the Circle E spread came into view.

Pat Wilkes scanned the area as they approached the ranch buildings. John Gideon Shaw looked expectantly for signs of Sam. His face clouded with concern. Sam should have been there to welcome them. Captain Tom Evans may have been resting up with his rheumatism, but Sam would have been halfway across the yard to greet them by now.

The chuck wagon hauled to a halt outside the house. The door stood ajar. Pat Wilkes stepped down from his horse.

'There's something amiss here,' he said,

hurrying towards the open door. Entering the house, he spotted the body of Tom Evans on the floor.

'Beanpole,' the ramrod called urgently and the lanky cook was alongside him in a flash. The rest of the crew dismounted and stood waiting at the porch. The foreman knelt down beside the body and noticed the broad bloodstain on the Circle E owner's shirt.

'He's been shot, Buck,' Wilkes whispered, as he gently searched for any sign of life.

'He's still alive,' he said excitedly. 'Quick, get some hot water, Buck, and one of you men go find a blanket and, you, get the bottle of whiskey. Hurry.'

Grabbing John Gideon as he made to pass, Wilkes continued, 'See if you can find Sam. He might be able to shed some light on what's happened here.' The young man turned on his heels and sprinted out of the house and made for the outbuildings.

Buck Beanpole stoked up the stove and in no time at all he had some water heated and ready.

One of the crew was sent to town for the doctor while the other two helped the ramrod to ease Tom Evans onto a quickly provided mattress on the floor. Pat Wilkes helped the cook locate and bathe the wound though Buck concluded that it looked dangerously close to the old rancher's heart and needed urgent medical attention if Captain Tom was to survive. Carefully he packed the wound with clean cotton and bound it tight before covering the old rancher with a blanket.

Heavy footsteps sounded on the wooden porch and John Gideon staggered in through the open door, with what looked like a bundle of filthy rags in his arms. He gently lowered what he was carrying onto the floor.

'What the...' Buck Beanpole began as he came to his aid. The cook dropped to his knees beside the lacerated body of Sam, the wrangler. It was only when John Gideon straightened out the bloody bundle that Sam's face was revealed and recognized. His clothes had been ripped to shreds, his boots split open and his broken body was lacerated from shoulder to feet.

The rope round his body had cut into his flesh and his fingers had been severed where they had gripped the rope in an attempt to free himself.

The silent onlookers shuddered at the sight of the mangled body of the chief wrangler who had been a popular member of the ranch crew. John Gideon stood clench-fisted but dry-eyed. During the years he had been at the Circle E a close relationship had developed between him and the old wrangler, who had taught him all he needed to know about horse training and breeding. The shock of finding Sam's mangled body brought back memories to the young man of his own grandfather's death those years ago which had caused him to venture from farming into ranching.

Somehow, it was like losing his grand-father all over again. The old feelings of anger and revenge were stirring and, coldly, young John Gideon went to get a blanket. Without emotion he allowed Buck Beanpole to assist him as he gently washed the battered face and straightened the clothing as best he could. Finally, Sam, the wrangler, was wrapped in a blanket.

The crew member who had ridden out for help, returned with Doc Edison. Untying his medicine bag from the saddle of his mount, the doctor dismounted and hurried into the ranch house.

'I'm sorry for the delay, Pat,' he said breathlessly.

'Let's hope you're in time,' the ramrod replied, easing himself away from the rancher so that the doctor could study the patient. A quick check had the doctor shaking his head. 'You've done a good job, Pat,' he said, 'But there isn't much I can do here. I'll have to get the captain into town. You do know about the mayhem in Lee-ward, don't you?'

Pat Wilkes shook his head.

'We've just got back from the cattle drive.

Found Captain Evans shot and that's what's left of old Sam,' he said, pointing to the blanket-covered form on the floor. 'He was roped and dragged by whoever shot the captain and,' he added, glancing round the room, 'looks like they looted the place.'

'It must have been the gang who raided the town,' Doc Edison concluded, snapping his bag shut. 'Can you get Tom comfortable on a wagon? I don't think he has much of a chance but he's a tough old bird. If anyone can make it, he will.'

Buck Beanpole and the crew set to emptying the chuck wagon to make enough room for the old rancher. Pat Wilkes questioned the doctor about the raiders as he held his horse for mounting. John Gideon Shaw stood on the porch listening.

'Nobody knows who they were,' Doc Edison recounted. 'They just came in – about ten of them – robbed the bank, the saloon, the stores ... anyone who saw their faces or got in their way they just shot ... men, women, didn't matter to them. They even shot two of the saloon girls after they had given their favours.'

Buck Beanpole stepped down from the wagon and over to the doctor.

'Who in the saloon? Which women, Doc?' he asked.

The doctor shook his head. 'I don't rightly know which of them was killed, I was too busy with the wounded. All I know is there were two killed, shot dead.' The doctor climbed aboard his horse. 'I can't stay here jawing, there's much to be done. Get Tom Evans into town. I'll be waiting for him.' He spurred his horse and headed for Leeward.

Buck Beanpole followed with the wagon with John Gideon and Pat Wilkes riding alongside.

The job of cleaning up the house and preparing a burial site for Sam was left in the capable hands of the other members of the crew.

Buck stopped the wagon outside the doctor's surgery. Doc Edison was there waiting, ready to operate. His wife, who was a trained nurse, stood expectantly alongside him.

'Get Tom inside. Careful now. Leave him with me and go get yourselves a stiff drink and something to eat. I reckon you've earned it. I'll send for you later.'

His suggestion suited the three men who silently made their way to the saloon, passing windows that were newly boarded up or in various stages of repair. Inside the saloon the atmosphere was very subdued. Before Buck Beanpole could ask the barman any questions about the saloon girls, he was told that his favourite, Nell, was dead and lying in the undertaker's with the others.

The lanky cook made no direct comment, just took the proffered bottle of whiskey and slumped down at a table. Young Shaw collected the glasses and joined him having been informed that Meg's café had been shot up. Meg, the owner, had been killed and the young waitress for whom John Gideon had a shine on could not be found.

In silence, Buck Beanpole poured three large drinks and glanced across to the bar, to where Pat Wilkes was deep in conversation. The bottle was half empty by the time the ramrod joined his friends to verify what the doctor had told them. The bank manager and teller had been shot and killed. Shops had been raided and blasted and many people had been shot as the gang rode away. He lowered his voice as he confirmed what John Gideon already knew about the death of the café owner and the missing girl.

Perhaps the worst news was that not one person could give a description of any of the gang that could prove helpful, other than to say that they thought there were ten in number.

It was dark when Doctor Edison came through the saloon doors. The three Circle E riders still sat at the same table. The whiskey bottle was nearly empty and the remains of a meal was strewn across the table. Pat Wilkes stood up as he spotted the doctor glancing around the room.

'Over here, Doc. How's the Captain?' he asked.

'I got the bullet out but I'm not too happy about him. We'll have to wait and see what develops,' the doctor said, picking up the whiskey bottle and draining the remaining liquid. 'I needed that, Pat,' he sighed with satisfaction, before continuing, 'This business will have to be reported to the Rangers.'

'Hasn't anyone sent a telegraph?' Wilkes asked.

'We can't. They shot up the lines.'

John Gideon seemed to spring to life. 'I'll ride out,' he said, pushing back his chair.

Buck Beanpole urged him to sit down. 'You're in no fit condition to go anywhere, young fella. You'll just get yourself all fired up and who knows when we'll see you again?' he said.

'Buck's right, John Gideon, I reckon we'll be needing all the help we can get on the Circle E, what with Sam gone,' Pat Wilkes added.

'We'll send Johnson to alert the Texas Rangers when we get back,' the cook added, naming one of the riders from the ranch.

'No, Buck. Sorry Pat, I've made up my mind. I'm riding to tell Jack Hart. He'll want to know about the boss and he might know something about these raiders. The sooner we find out...'

Buck Beanpole saw it was useless to argue with the young man. The look in his eyes told him not to. Pat Wilkes broke the silence. 'OK, son, but wait till morning, till you're more sober.'

'No. I'm OK, boss. I'll go back to the ranch with you to collect one or two things I'm likely to need but I've wasted too much time already.'

The three men left the saloon with the doctor who promised to let them know how the ranch owner was progressing. He watched the two riders climb aboard their horses and escort the wagon as they left town at a steady pace to return to the Circle E.

At the ranch, they were met by the rest of the crew who were eager to know how Captain Evans was. The journey back had not altered John Gideon's determination to be on his way as soon as possible.

'There's been enough time wasted,' he argued as he unsaddled his horse.

'What about Sam? Ain't you stayin' for his burial?' one of the crew asked.

'Sure,' sighed John Gideon. 'Let's do it.'

And so it was that their old friend Sam was buried by lantern light, while Pat Wilkes muttered something from the Bible about God and care. When the grave was best part filled in, John Gideon slammed down his spade, jammed his hat on his head and returned to the bunkhouse. Stuffing a few necessities in his warbag, he slung his saddle-bags over his shoulder and made his way to the stable where he began to saddle his big grulla. Buck Beanpole appeared with a bundle of food and without a word being exchanged, John Gideon left the cook to tie it to the back of the grulla's saddle while he went to get his rifle.

Buck watched his friend as he returned and booted the Sharps .50 before checking all was ready for his departure. Stepping forward, he grabbed the big young man by the shoulder. 'Don't go off on your own, son. When you've seen Hart come back here.'

Young Shaw shook his head. 'I can't promise anything,' he said, leading his horse out of the stable before climbing aboard. The grulla snorted and stamped its feet, eager to be off. The power of his favourite horse felt reassuring. Turning to the lanky cook he said, 'Somebody must pay for this, Buck, and they will.'

The big animal set off, fresh and eager to get going. John Gideon's thoughts were of the dead wrangler, Sam, and how he had taught him all about horses. He could hear his voice, see him working the remuda. Urging his grulla to greater speed, John Gideon tightened his muscles and felt the big Sharps .50 under his leg. He patted the bulge in his saddle-bags where the shot and powder for his home-made bullets lay. He thought of the torn and mangled body.

'I'll find them, Sam,' he vowed. 'Jack Hart will tell me how.'

Jack Hart, the Texas Ranger, was an old colleague and close friend of both young Shaw and Captain Evans. He would advise him. Sure and steady, that was Jack Hart, and that, John Gideon knew, would be his advice. The pace slackened somewhat as the rider's anger was levelled with reason and he concentrated on the task in hand. He knew the trail well and the bright moonlit night helped the horse and rider eat up the miles. He only stopped long enough to rest his horse, make coffee and have a quick snack before riding off again into the night, the big grulla loping at a steady pace it could maintain for long periods.

It was a tired young man and beast who pulled up outside the livery stable in Austin, the next day. John Gideon put his horse into the stable, paid the ostler two dollars for the best service and walked stiffly to the Texas Rangers' office.

Jack Hart looked up from his desk as the door of his office was rapped sharply and opened. His face broke into a smile as he recognized the big frame of John Gideon Shaw standing in the doorway, but straightened when he saw the serious look on the young man's face and the gunrig about his hips.

'What's brought you here, young fella? And why so serious?' Jack Hart said, extending his right hand stiffly as he came round from behind his desk. Shaw took his hand and looked deeply into the eyes of the ageing ranger. It was a while since he had seen his old friend who had been promoted to a desk job since being shot up and badly wounded two years earlier in Capstan.

'Can I sit down Jack, I've been in the saddle since yesterday?'

Hart pulled out a chair, gesturing for his young friend to be seated. He poured a mug of coffee from the pot simmering on the stove in the corner. John Gideon took a sip of the black liquid before beginning to explain what had happened. Jack Hart listened intently only interrupting to ask about his friend, Captain Tom Evans.

'Where do you think the murdering rats will be?' Shaw asked.

'They'll be miles away by now, probably riding close to the border,' the ranger said. 'There are a number of gangs roaming all over the West. They are mostly deserters or ex-soldiers who can't settle after the war. Some have come back home to find their farms razed to the ground, their wives dead or gone off with someone else while they were away. All they want to do is kill and rob. They been trained for it.' He poured fresh coffee before asking, 'Don't suppose any names were mentioned?'

John Gideon shook his head. 'They were strangers to the town. They went where they knew money was likely to be, took it and shot the people they robbed and any witnesses. Only thing for sure we know is that they travelled past the Circle E on their way out.'

'I'll send a man out,' Jack Hart said. 'If he comes up with anything, I'll let you know.'

John Gideon Shaw shook his head, 'No Jack, that's not good enough. I need to do this. I'd like my badge back.'

The old ranger stared at John Gideon. The cold mask of hatred that he had last seen years ago, when he had first met the young man, was back. Jack Hart opened the drawer in the desk. Picking out a badge, he rubbed its surface on his shirt and scrutinized his young visitor.

'Are you sure you're up to the task, my friend? It's been quite a while since you've been on the tracking trail. You're sure to be a bit rusty. A bit like this badge I shouldn't wonder,' he added, squinting at the star before tossing it to his seated friend. He smiled as Shaw adeptly caught it. 'Put that in your pocket. Show it only when need be and remember, it's of no use south of the border.'

'Thanks, Jack.'

'Captain to you now, Shaw, you're a ranger.' They both stood up and shook hands.

'If you want my advice. Go get some food and rest and report back here before you leave.'

John Gideon saluted his senior and leaving the office strode over to the boarding house used by the Texas Rangers.

THREE

Next day, refreshed and with Captain Jack Hart's parting gift of a new Winchester repeater replacing his other carbines, John Gideon set off for the Mexican border. He went along with what Jack Hart had suggested – that he make a sweep of the border towns, stopping only long enough to pick up any gossip or information on the comings and goings of the most recent visitors. Five miles across the border he came to the first Mexican town, La Cruz. With virtually nothing to go on, John Gideon knew he must just keep his eyes and ears open while he hung about for a spell, searching for any sign of the gang.

His eyes scanned the length of the town. Most of the old buildings sat either side of the main street and were all, bar one, single storey constructions of adobe walls topped with a wooden roof. The largest building was the cantina, with its railed off board-walk. Further to the edge of the town the houses were set back somewhat with vegetable plots and flower patches behind picket fencing. Opposite the cantina was the only two-storey building, which a quick glance in the window confirmed was the town store. Shaw's attention was drawn to the twitch of a curtain in the upper storey and he saw a young woman staring down at him. She smiled flirtatiously and he dropped his glance as he dismounted.

The young woman's eyes followed John Gideon till he entered the building then her face vanished to be replaced by a man's, whose quizzical gaze focused on the big grulla that stood outside the cantina. The man swivelled his gaze up and down the street before turning his attention back to the half-naked woman behind him.

'What did the rider look like?' he grated.

She shrugged herself into a cotton dress.

'He was a tall *hombre* – very young and very handsome,' she said, eyeing her client, who was pulling on his shirt. 'You have finished with me now, *señor?*' she asked.

The man, whose name was Grady, nodded. 'Yeah, for now. I've a thirst needs quenching and a curiosity needs satisfying. Reckon I'll take a look at this *hombre*. You stay put, d'ye hear.'

The woman scooped the money he had left her into a drawer before going to the window to watch Grady cross to the cantina. He studied the mount tied at the hitching rail and noticed the empty rifle boot. Once again, he looked up and down the street before pushing the door open and entering the cantina. The young woman watching sighed and glanced along to the right and studied the small building further up the street from the cantina. She noted that the curtains were drawn and concluded that the two friends of Grady, whom she had entertained earlier, must be having a siesta. She yawned and went and lay on the bed. Her friend, who lived in a neighbouring village, had been sent for and would be here soon. Till then, she would rest and be bright and eager for her batch of clients. The three men had ridden into the town two days ago with money they were eager to spend. She dozed off with a contented smile on her face.

Across the street, Grady had entered the cantina. In the shadowy light he saw the tall stranger standing at the bar. He looked about. Three Mexicans sat at a table playing poker with a tattered pack of cards. They ignored Grady as he strode over to the bar and stood by John Gideon Shaw. Shaw looked at Grady and feigned a look of surprise. Picking up his glass of beer, he saluted him with, 'I didn't expect to see a fellow American, hereabouts,' before swallowing a good draught and adding, 'Can I buy you a drink?'

Grady acknowledged the greeting and accepted the invitation of a drink.

'Do you live here?' asked Shaw, waiting till

Grady lowered his glass.

'Just staying over for a time,' Grady replied, eyeing the big stranger and noticing the tied down gun on his hip and the Winchester repeater leaning against the bar.

'And you. You looking for work?' Grady asked him.

'Not down here, I ain't.'

Grady waited for more conversation but the young stranger just smiled and remained silent.

'You're carrying some hardware. That there one of those newfangled rifles?' Grady ventured, nodding towards the Winchester.

'Reckon it is,' Shaw replied, hoisting it across his forearm.

Grady sniggered. 'Making sure you get what you're after, I take it?'

'I need it in my job,' Shaw replied, and his tone was a few degrees colder.

The smile left Grady's countenance. 'What exactly is your job? You some kind of bounty hunter?'

John Gideon remained silent and Grady's

inquisitive look turned to one of wariness. 'Who are you looking for?' he asked. 'I may be able to help you.'

'There's nobody I want over here,' John Gideon said. 'You could say I'm here for a holiday.'

Grady winked knowingly, 'You want to hole up for a while?' He finished his drink and ordered another. 'You'll have one with me?'

John Gideon nodded. 'Don't mind if I do.'

Hefting his rifle and picking up his drink, he nodded to a table against the back wall. 'Let's sit. Perhaps you could tell me a bit about this place. You seem to know your way around here.'

'There's not much to tell,' Grady said, as the two men settled themselves. 'Good place to rest up – cheap and obliging – as long as you mind your own business. Most trade is just passing through. Only thing to pass the time is drink and the local whore. It might improve when the other soiled dove *lands* sometime today or tomorrow.' He spluttered in his beer as he laughed at his last remark.

'You on your own?' John Gideon asked.

'No, there's three of us,' Grady answered, wiping his chin with the back of his hand and glancing at his drinking partner. 'We're resting, so to speak. A bit like yourself.'

John Gideon thought it best to steer away from further personal questioning and asked Grady's advice about where and what to eat. After a while, their conversation dried up and their glasses were empty.

Grady reached inside his vest pocket and pulled out his watch.

'Time to go. I promised to wake my two pards about now. See you around if you're staying over.'

Grady rose as he pocketed the watch and with a final nod to his seated companion, left the cantina. John Gideon sat grim-faced, both his hands clamped tightly round his empty glass. He had had to will himself to stay calm and amenable. He pulled the air in through his nostrils and breathed in deeply and slowly his tension eased. It had taken a lot of control to stop himself from shooting Grady on the spot when he saw the watch his drinking partner had sported.

He had recognized it instantly as belonging to his old employer, Tom Evans, who lay critically ill in Leeward.

So, Grady was one of the raiders who had been responsible for the mayhem in Leeward and involved in the shooting of the Circle E ranch owner and the death of Sam. If Grady had been the only one involved, John Gideon would have shot him there and then in the cantina, but the raider was here in La Cruz with two of the others. Captain Jack Hart's advice came to mind: sure and steady. Killing the three, in haste, was not the solution. There would still be seven more on the loose and Shaw intended to find every one of the raiders. Grady would lead him to them.

Young Shaw's expression relaxed though his eyes were still as sharp and cold as steel. He cradled the Winchester as he strolled over to the door and looked over the top of it. Grady had walked down the street and was about to enter one of the buildings further along. Shaw watched long enough to make sure he entered the dwelling before returning to the bar.

The stocky Mexican bar-owner reached for an empty glass. John Gideon shook his head. 'No more,' he said. 'Where would I get a room?'

The man came from behind the bar and walked to the door. He pointed to the store opposite, 'One?' he stuck up a finger. 'One *hombre?*'

John Gideon nodded and continued, 'Where can I get my horse stabled?' pointing to his grulla.

The bar-owner walked to the corner of the cantina. Gesturing with the same finger, he indicated to the rear of the cantina, to a large wooden shed with a broken fence around it.

'OK?' he asked, holding out his hand for money.

John Gideon looked at the Mexican who smiled at him with raised eyebrows and shoulders. He smiled and nodded as he fumbled in his pocket before placing a coin in the open palm. The Mexican turned on his heels and returned to his bar.

John Gideon collected his warbag and walked across the street. If there was a room available there it would be an ideal spot to watch the place where the three raiders were staying and keep an eye on the cantina. He entered the store and the smells of pungent herbs and coffee tickled his nostrils. Canned goods lined the shelves. Leaning on the counter with hands widespread was the storekeeper.

'Have you a room?' John Gideon asked.

The storekeeper nodded. *'Si, señor.* One?' The man's finger stood up.

It seemed to be the town's favoured method of communication, Shaw thought, as he returned the gesture.

'One,' he confirmed, indicated himself with his thumb. 'Can I have something to eat?' he asked, pointing to his mouth.

The storekeeper nodded, '*Si señor. Si.* I will cook it and bring it to you.'

His English was very good and John Gideon wondered why all the finger gesturing was needed. Perhaps the town inhabitants had their own reasons for it.

'You want woman?'

John Gideon shook his head. 'No, not now. Later perhaps. I'd like to see the room.'

The shopkeeper took him upstairs and pointed to the second door on the landing. As he passed the first door it opened. A woman stood framed in the doorway. She was young, attractive and partly clad in a flimsy dress. The sleepy look and dishevelled hair told him she had been roused from her afternoon siesta. He returned her smile and walked on to his room. Placing his rifle and warbag on the bed, he glanced around. It was a clean room, sparsely furnished with a bed, a cupboard and a chair. A basin and pitcher of water stood on top of the cupboard and a pitted mirror hung on the wall behind it. A towel lay over the chair. It would do.

Locking the door he retraced his steps downstairs and left the store to tend to his horse.

He guided his grulla to the shed at the rear of the cantina. The inside of the makeshift stable already held three other horses. He checked them for signs of ownership. One had an S on its rear. The others were un-branded. This did not surprise John Gideon and he surmised they belonged to the raiders.

There was plenty of hay and water available and John Gideon quickly settled his grulla. He felt his own guts begin to rumble as he tended his horse's needs and, leaving the grulla tied on a loose rope, he toted his gear and went back to the store. The owner met him with a tray containing a mess of beans and minced beef, home-made pancakes and a jug of coffee and offered to carry it up to his room. It smelt good and appetising and John Gideon realized how

54

hungry he was as he followed the store owner up the stairs and stepped ahead to open the door. Once ensconced comfortably in his room, he ate hungrily. The food was better than he thought it would be and it was soon gone, quickly followed by the coffee. He opened the room door and placed the tray on the floor outside. He glanced along the landing and listened. No sound came from the other room. The young woman was probably resting, he decided, getting herself ready for her evening's work. He re-entered his room and closed the door quietly. Perhaps he should follow her example he decided and, locking the door, the young ranger stretched out his big frame on the bed and still cradling the Winchester, closed his eyes and slept.

FOUR

It was early evening when he woke up. He poured the tepid water into the bowl and began his ablutions. He was shaving off a slight growth of beard when the door rattled. He grabbed the towel and patted his face as he turned the key. Grady, hair slickered down, stood outside still wearing the same soiled clothes.

'The barkeep said you were dossing here. I just knocked to tell you we're over in the cantina. Come and join us when you're ready, the boys want to meet you.'

'Sure. Just get myself something substantial to eat before I start on the liquor,' Shaw answered amicably.

'Right. Oh, and if we're not there, we'll be in the *casa* down the street – the barkeep knows where. Just follow the noises,' he sniggered. 'That other dove's arrived, so there's two to choose from.'

Young Shaw smiled. 'Don't let me keep you. I'll be over later.' Grady laughed coarsely as he strode off.

John Gideon closed the door and, having completed his ablutions, turned his attention to his Navy Colt. Drawing it from the belt on the bedrail he broke it open letting the shells fall on to the bed. He studied each one as he cleaned and replaced them in the cylinder. Tying on the belt, he slipped his gun into the holster and, watching his face in the mirror, practised drawing it. A quick hand, a steady eye and no telltale facial clues to signal his intent were his main aims.

A gentle knock on the door interrupted him.

'Come in,' he called, with his back to the door. He heard the door open and he spun round to see the storekeeper carrying food and coffee on a tray.

The Mexican stood transfixed in shock at

the sight of the gun pointed at his middle and the cold look of death in the young man's stare.

'*Señor!*' he gasped and the tray began to shake. John Gideon tossed the gun onto the bed and apologized. Smiling sheepishly, he took the tray of food and placed that on the bed too. Taking a few dollars from his pocket he handed them to the nervous storeman.

'Didn't mean to scare you. Just routine practising,' John Gideon explained, 'If there's more money needed, just say so.'

'No, *señor,* that is enough,' the Mexican stammered and left the room hastily.

John Gideon enjoyed the snack. The food and coffee were good. He stood by the window watching the street. He heard the door of the room next to his slam shut and female voices shrill with laughter interspersed with banter as they descended the stairs. Moving to the window, he saw two women cross from the store and enter the cantina. Dusk was beginning to fall but

Shaw refrained from lighting a lamp. He remained at the window and shortly afterwards the women reappeared with Grady and his two cohorts. Grady carried an armful of bottles. The two whores were laughing loudly at the mauling attention they were getting from Grady's two pals. The group strolled along the street to the adobe building where Grady and his two friends were staying. John Gideon stood watching them from the window till they disappeared inside. Grunting with satisfaction, he finished off the rest of the coffee. He was ready. One final check before he left. Adjusting his Navy Colt, he drew it and replaced it. The movement was smooth and quick.

Picking up the tray he went downstairs and, finding the store empty, he placed the tray on the counter and stepped outside. Standing in the shadowy doorway, he scanned the street. The house lights were flickering on as the sun set and darkness took its place. The town was quiet as if waiting for something to happen now that the Americanos had arrived.

John Gideon crossed to the cantina, bought a bottle of whiskey, made his way to the adobe *casa* down the street, and knocked politely. Grady, glass in hand, opened the door and welcomed him in. Shaw passed the bottle to him.

'Come in. Glad you decided to call,' Grady said, taking the bottle and ushering him in. From the back room, the giggling voices of the two women could be heard above the grunting and coarse remarks from Grady's two henchmen. Grady found an empty glass and pulled the whiskey cork as the back room door flew open. One of the men staggered across to the table, grabbed the glass and whiskey bottle from Grady, poured himself a drink, returned the bottle with a sickly grin and re-entered the room. Not a word was spoken. Grady laughed as the man vanished.

'Boyd's in a hurry to get back to it,' he said, sliding a fresh glass and the whiskey bottle to Shaw.

John Gideon poured himself a drink and sipped at the liquid.

'It's our turn next and the new girl's as good a looker as the other one,' Grady grinned, putting his glass down and rubbing his hands together. 'This sure is the good life,' he said, stumbling to a chair and plonking himself down. 'You can stay here if you want and ride out with us when we leave. I've talked it over with Jansen and Boyd and they're in agreement.'

It was evident to John Gideon that Grady had swallowed a fair amount of liquor. He decided to ask a few more questions and try to find out where the rest of the gang was.

'How long are you staying here for?'

Grady humped his shoulders. 'A month. Till the money runs out or a job turns up. It depends.'

The bedroom door jerked open and Jansen and Boyd came back into the room where Grady sat with Shaw.

'They sure are a pair of goers, Grady,' one

of the men began, before spotting John Gideon Shaw and stopping to look him over.

'So you're the gunny Grady was telling us about,' he said, pouring himself a drink. 'Don't recognize your face from anywheres. What's your name?' He straightened up, looking at John Gideon, with bleary, slightly suspicious eyes.

'My name's John Gideon,' the young man answered, standing up and politely offering his hand. 'And what do I call you?'

'Boyd,' the man replied, 'and this here's Jansen.' A more congenial look crossed Boyd's face as he pumped the proffered hand of John Gideon Shaw. 'Welcome to the company,' he grinned. 'Now go on in and have some fun. There's nothing like sharing a good whore or two to firm up a friendship.' Grady stood up, swayed for a moment, then lurched towards the bedroom.

John Gideon followed in his wake. If he wanted to be accepted by the three men he had to take what he was offered.

The women were lying, drinking liquor, on single cots which were separated by a small cupboard. Grady stumbled over to the new woman, tossing his shirt to one side.

'*Dinero* first, please, *señor*,' the woman said, pointing to the money that had been left by Jansen and Boyd.

Grady pulled a wad of money from his pants pocket and tossed a few more dollars onto the pile. John Gideon did likewise only his contribution was smaller. Grady laughed drunkenly. 'You're in the wrong job,' he told Shaw, shaking the roll of money in the young man's face, before pocketing it.

'Well, I'll work along with you if the offer still stands,' Shaw said.

'We'll talk about it later. Right now I've other things on my mind,' Grady slurred, reaching roughly for the yielding softness of the soiled dove. John Gideon followed suit, taking what was offered, though his mind was on revenge and not the woman beneath him, who, for all he was barely aware of, did her job very well.

Grady's grunts changed to snores and the sound of his sleeping was a signal for John Gideon to rise and get dressed. The two girls scooped up their money and followed John Gideon out of the bedroom. Stopping only to confirm a time for their future services, they left their clients with cheerful banter. They had been well paid for their services and at that moment were happy, richer and intoxicated.

When they left, John Gideon Shaw sat for a while talking with the two raiders. Finally he posed the proposition – 'Grady mentioned that you could use me on your next job.'

Boyd nodded. 'Yes, we might be able to use you, but it's not up to us.'

'What do you mean?' Shaw probed.

Jansen butted in, 'I think you've said enough,' he said to Boyd.

John Gideon wanted more information and pushed for it. 'There's more than you three?' he queried, turning his attention to

Jansen. The outlaw nodded, but remained tight lipped.

'It's just that Grady said–'

'Leave it for now,' Jansen said, getting to his feet and opening the door. 'We'll talk in the morning.'

John Gideon nodded. He did not want to push his luck. He had become acquainted with the three gang members, which was quite an achievement in such a short time.

'See you tomorrow then,' he said and stepping through the front entrance, headed towards his lodgings.

The small town was quiet as he made his way back to the store and his room. John Gideon Shaw swilled himself down before finally climbing into bed, where he tossed restlessly with the image of the torn and bloodied body of Sam the wrangler on his mind and the hand of the killer Grady, holding the captain's watch. Tomorrow could not come quick enough for John Gideon Shaw. It would be a day of retribution for his three new acquaintances.

FIVE

The probing fingers of early morning sunlight woke John Gideon Shaw. He squinted himself awake and tossed the blanket from the bed. Going to the water jug he poured some into the bowl and swilled his face and body in the cold, invigorating liquid, before rubbing himself dry with the rough towel.

Alerted by the sound of footsteps shuffling outside the room door, he paused and waited. A light knock followed by *'señor?'* identified the caller and John Gideon opened the door to find the owner nervously holding his breakfast. The coffee shook on the tray.

'Your food, *señor,*' the owner said, smiling with relief at finding a towel and not a gun in the young man's hand.

'*Gracias,*' John Gideon said, making way for the owner to enter and put the tray on the bedside locker. The Mexican hurried away leaving his guest to eat his breakfast.

Young Shaw set a chair by the window, and placing the tray on his knee he proceeded to demolish the food and drink while he studied the buildings and street below him. The town was quiet and the main thoroughfare was empty. There was no need for folks to rise too early in a place like this border town. John Gideon heard a door open outside on the landing and the high-pitched voices of the two whores as they left the room. He focused his gaze downward, watching the front of the boarding house. He saw the two women appear on the street and watched them hurry across the road and down to the adobe building that he surmised still housed the three gang members. The door opened to their knocking and they hurried inside.

John Gideon left the window and picked up his gun-belt. Buckling it on, he checked the cylinder load in his gun and spun it before replacing it in his holster. Packing his few belongings into his warbag, he left the room and walked down the stairs. At the sound of his footsteps the Mexican appeared from the back room. Approaching the counter John Gideon smiled and tossed him his loose change. *'Gracias,'* he said. 'That was a good meal.' A nervous nod was the only answer he got as the Mexican's fingers folded over the coins and his eyes watched the tall, loose-limbed young man walk out of the shop. Pocketing the coins, the shop owner went upstairs to the vacant room to collect the tray and tidy the room. He grunted with satisfaction as he started to remake the bed. It was good enough for the next rider who came over the border seeking a place to rest and hide before moving on.

Young Shaw made his way to the stable. Saddling up his big grulla, he secured his warbag and, taking a length of rope he found in the stable, he coiled it and hooked it on his saddle.

'Won't be long now, old fella,' he confided, patting the big horse's neck. 'Just a little while longer.'

Leaving the stable, he went back to the main street and took a seat outside the canteen. His eyes were angled down the street towards the *casa* where the two women were presumably entertaining the three killers. His thoughts were on those three men. John Gideon had made up his mind. He did not have time to wait two or three weeks before leaving here with Grady and his sidekicks. He had decided to kill them now and move on to the next border town to search for the remainder of the gang.

It was nearly two hours later when the women emerged, smiling and chattering as they headed for their room above the store. They spotted John Gideon Shaw outside the cantina.

'*Hola, señor.*'

He acknowledged their greetings. One of them swirled, her skirts lifting high on her tanned thighs.

'You would like some, *señor?*' she called teasingly.

'Later,' he replied, as he rose from his seat to make his way down the street.

'You know where we are, *señor.* We will be waiting and if you get lost we will find you,' they giggled.

Ignoring their banter, John Gideon strode light-footedly on. He tried the door of the adobe *casa.* It opened to his touch and he stepped cautiously inside.

All three men looked up at the sound of the door opening. They were at the table eating breakfast.

'You should have come earlier. You could have had breakfast and a woman,' Jansen said. 'There's plenty of coffee. Get a cup from the back.'

'Yeah, help yourself,' Grady added. 'Them *señoritas* can make good coffee, too.'

Boyd went back to sopping up the remains of his breakfast with a crust of bread. He cleaned his plate and gulped it down with hot coffee.

71

John Gideon Shaw took a step forward and drew his Colt.

'Stand away from the table,' he said, his cold eyes staring at the three men.'

Boyd dropped his cup and the contents spilled over the table.

'What's your game?' Grady spluttered. The three remained seated, waiting for a reply.

It was Jansen who spoke next. 'You can see his game. He's come to take what money we have. I told you not to go yapping to strangers.'

'I don't want your money. I want information about the gang who raided Leeward, shot the owner of the Circle E ranch and horse-dragged the Negro wrangler.'

'We don't know nothing about any town or ranch owner,' Jansen said.

'You're a liar,' John Gideon said. 'What time is it Grady?'

'It's early,' Grady said nervously. 'What kind of a question's that?'

'Look at your timepiece.'

Grady fumbled in his pocket and looked at his watch. 'It's eleven-thirty.'

'Where did you get that watch?' John Gideon aimed his gun at Grady.

'I bought it,' Grady answered.

'That watch was stolen from Captain Tom Evans, the owner of the Circle E, when you shot him.'

Young Shaw's voice was low and cold.

Jansen, beside himself with anger, turned on Grady. 'You're a bigger fool than I thought, sporting that timepiece.' Both men leapt to their feet.

'Shut your face, Jansen,' Grady retorted. Jansen took a swing at Grady and knocked the watch from his grasp. It skidded across the table and into Shaw's waiting grasp.

'Quiet, both of you,' John Gideon interrupted. 'What I need to know now is where I can find the rest of your gang?'

'Go to hell,' Jansen snarled, turning to face the young man with the gun.

The Navy Colt jumped in John Shaw's fist. The lobe of Jansen's left ear vanished as the bullet ripped it off on its way to lodge in the adobe wall behind him. Jansen screamed, his hand clutched at the livid wound and blood ran freely into his clenched fist and down his arm.

Both men collapsed back on to their chairs.

'Now, I'll ask you again,' John Gideon said coldly and precisely, cutting through Jansen's whimpering. 'Where is the rest of the gang?' He cocked his gun and pointed it at Jansen's chest.

'Give me a chance. You wouldn't shoot an unarmed man.'

John Gideon looked at the three outlaws crouched nervously at the table. His eyes searched the room. He spotted a gunrig slung on a wall hook. Side-stepping over, he grabbed the belt with his free hand and tossed it high to Jansen.

'Put that on.'

The outlaw rose to his feet and caught the belt in both hands. The blood ran freely now down the side of his neck. Wiping the sticky blood from his fingers onto the front of his shirt, Jansen fumbled to fasten the gun-belt round his waist. When he had settled the gun he looked at John Gideon Shaw.

'Do I get a fair chance?' he asked, nodding to the Colt in Shaw's hand.

John Gideon replaced his gun in its holster. In that split second, Jansen thought he saw a chance to outdraw the young man before him. The throbbing pain from his ear was suddenly forgotten. He made a move for his gun as Shaw replaced his. His gun levelled. As it did so, John Shaw pulled the trigger of his gun. The slug hit Jansen in the face and the outlaw was dead before he hit the floor.

Grady and Boyd gasped at the speed of hand of the young man before them. One minute his gun was being replaced in its holster, the next it was exploding and Jansen's face was transformed as the lead missile hit home. The smoking gun was then pointed towards Jansen's companions.

'You, stand up,' Shaw nodded to Boyd.

The outlaw slowly got to his feet.

'Get that gun-belt and put it on.'

'No. I won't. I can't equal that.' Boyd felt for the chair at the table and made to sit down. The gun exploded again. Blood flowed from his chest as the bullet struck home. Boyd looked down at the burgeoning red stain on his shirt. He shook his head and mouthed 'No' and the chair fell back under his slumped body.

Grady darted for the bedroom door. He stumbled as the gun again exploded. An excruciating pain ran through his leg as the bullet wrecked his knee. Screaming, he crawled along the floor. He reached for the door jamb. John Gideon stepped forward and dealt him a swift blow behind the ear with his pistol, silencing the last of the outlaws. Pocketing the watch, Shaw quickly stepped over to the door and onto the main street. A number of townsfolk had gathered outside the cantina looking down to where the sound of shots had emanated. None of them moved as John Gideon strode past on his way to collect his horse and that of Grady. They remained watchful but aloof as he retraced his steps back to the adobe *casa*. Dragging Grady's unconscious body from the house, he unceremoniously heaved it across the saddle and tied it down with the rope he had found in the stable. Satisfied that his quarry was secure for the moment, Shaw re-entered the *casa* and searched both the dead inhabitants and the squalid rooms. His search was fruitful and he recovered a great deal of cash which was the stolen property of the townsfolk of Leeward. Stuffing all but a handful of dollars into saddle-bags, he left the house and, slinging the saddle-bags in front of him, mounted his grulla and set off back up the main street, towing Grady's mount behind his own.

The two whores, who had so recently laughed and bantered with the outlaws and John Gideon Shaw, now stood silent and wide-eyed in the open doorway of the town store, their shawls drawn close around their ample contours.

Reining in alongside of them, John Gideon reached down and proffered them the loose dollars.

'There's enough there to bury those two sidewinders I left in the *casa*. What's left is yours,' he said.

The boldest one stepped forward. *'Gracias, señor.* You will come again, *si?'*

Young Shaw smiled grimly and signalled his grulla forward.

The group outside the cantina began to drift away. Only the two women stayed to watch the rider and his captive companion leave La Cruz.

Once outside of town, the grulla set off at an even pace with the second horse following obediently behind despite the unresponsive burden on its back. As Grady began to regain consciousness the searing throb in his knee was accentuated by the movement of the horse beneath him. He gasped and let out a strangled cry of pain.

Ahead, the grulla's ears pricked and for a moment his gait changed. Calming his mount, Shaw turned in the saddle to see the wild-eyed Grady foaming at the mouth as he tried to call out.

The young ranger slowed his horse and once he had gained a fairly secluded area he stopped and dismounted.

Untying his captive he unceremoniously dumped him on the ground.

'My leg. You've shattered my leg,' Grady complained.

'Let me see,' proffered Shaw, stooping down to straighten the outlaw's legs. Grady did not resist. Deftly, John Gideon looped the rope he now held round the ankle of the injured leg and stepping over to his horse, proceeded to tie it to the cantle.

'What are you doing?' Grady gasped in panic.

'Helping you regain your memory. Let's see now, what time is it?' With that he took Captain Tom Evans's timepiece from his pocket and dangled it over Grady's face.

'Wait. Don't. I'll tell you what you want to know.'

'What do I want to know?' John Gideon asked.

'About the watch. You were right. I did take it from the old rancher but I didn't shoot him. It was Embrel – Embrel shot him ... and Wilson, a man named Wilson dragged the Negro. You'll find him up north somewhere ... in one of the towns along the border.'

'Who runs the gang and where do I find him?' John Gideon asked.

'Embrel's the leader ... Ned Embrel ... he's the one runs the gang. Now he's one you'll have to look out for. Don't care who he kills. Even killed one of the whores in Leeward. Now there's an *hombre* you should be after.' Grady stopped for breath, his eyes raised and pleading.

'And where does this Embrel hang out?' The questioner remained cold and detached.

'All over. The gang meets in a month's time at San Credo. Then we'll ride out again.' He lay still waiting to see what

Shaw's reaction would be to the information he had given him.

John Gideon Shaw nodded his head. He did not remove the rope immediately.

'Let me loose. I've told you all I know,' Grady said. He reached down and tried to undo his bound feet. Shaw pushed him back with his foot.

'Roll over,' he commanded. Grady did as he was bid and the young ranger untied the rope and stepped away and told Grady to take off his shirt and use it to dress his own wound. That done, Grady was roughly handled back onto his horse with his hands firmly fixed to his saddle.

Satisfied that his captive was secure, John Gideon climbed aboard his big grulla and headed back for Austin to deliver his prisoner and to pass on to Jack Hart the future plans of Ned Embrel and his gang.

SIX

Ranger Captain Jack Hart stood by his office door with a puzzled look on his face. He had taken a walk round town to loosen his aching joints that had stiffened while doing his office work. Now his attention was focused on the two riders coming into view at the edge of town and slowly travelling along the main street of Austin towards him. One was sitting tall and easy, the other was rocking back and forth. It was evident to the old ranger that the rocking man was tied into his saddle and that his mount was being guided by the tall rider in front. It did not take him long to recognize his friend John Gideon Shaw.

As the pair halted outside the ranger's office, Captain Jack Hart stepped down from the boardwalk onto the dirt street to meet and greet the young ranger. John Gideon leaned down and shook the extended hand of his superior before stepping stiffly down from his mount to swing his saddle-bags over his shoulder.

'Good to see you back, son,' Jack Hart said, as he glanced across at the second horse and rider. The slumping form of the outlaw Grady swayed forward and his horse stepped nervously backward and forward. Jack Hart grabbed the reins and called over his shoulder for Biggs, his helper, to come and give a hand. The ranger captain noted Shaw's indifference as the young man strode into the office. He studied the bound outlaw – as he waited for Biggs to join him – his ashen pallor and the bloodied, torn trousers. Biggs helped him to undo the rope that held Grady on his horse and the outlaw moaned as he was hauled from his horse and carried into the rangers' headquarters.

'You better go get the doctor and bring him here,' Jack Hart said to Biggs, as they laid Grady on the office floor. The outlaw lapsed into unconsciousness and Hart turned his attention to John Gideon. 'Sit down, son,' he said, indicating the spare chair at his desk, 'Reckon you could do with a refresher before you tell me what I need to know.' Moving the heavy saddle-bags from the table to the floor, he proceeded to pour the young ranger a generous helping of liquor from his special reserve supply. Sliding the glass slowly across to John Gideon he lifted his eyebrows in silent query, nodding towards the outlaw lying unconscious on the floor. The old ranger listened as his young friend told him what had happened in the border town. Shaw was well into his retelling of events when the town doctor arrived. Without formality, or even asking a question, the doctor knelt down beside the wounded man and began inspecting Grady's condition.

'There's not much I can do with his leg,' he declared brusquely, interrupting the lawmen's conversation. 'It's a very bad wound and it's infected. It looks like an amputation job to me.'

The doctor looked around. 'You don't mind if I borrow Biggs a while to move this patient to the surgery?' and without waiting for an answer addressed the waiting man. 'Biggs go over and get Marvin and the stretcher.' He stooped down once more to tend to Grady.

John Gideon finished his story without further interruption.

'So, you got three of them. That leaves seven still roaming along the border towns,' Hart commented.

John Gideon nodded his head wearily.

'There's two groups by the sound of it – a party of four and the other's a threesome. A man named Embrel is the leader.'

Jack Hart added the name to his notes recording all that John Gideon said.

'You think they will be linking up again in the near future?'

'If what Grady says is right and there's a month between raids the next one's about due in three weeks' time.'

Grady moaned as the doctor temporarily bandaged the infected leg wound.

Jack Hart went and stood over him.

'How is he, Doctor? Is he fit enough to answer some questions?'

'I doubt he's fit enough to breathe,' the doctor commented drily, 'but you can try.'

'Now then Grady listen up,' Hart urged softly. 'Your welfare depends on your co-operating.'

The raider opened his eyes wearily and looked first at Jack Hart then over to John Gideon.

Hart read out the notes he had made, then paused to look deep into the outlaw's eyes.

'Well, is that right? Can you confirm that?' he asked Grady, who lay silent and breathing shallowly. 'It's in your best interests to tell us the truth. The doctor here is a good man but outlaws try his patience somewhat. A few words from you can help steady the doctor's hand and keep his temper cool and calm. You understand what I'm saying?'

With laboured breath, Grady confirmed

that Embrel was the leader and that the gang were due to get together in a town called San Credo in about three weeks' time.

Biggs and Marvin returned with the stretcher and the doctor and the rangers watched in silence as they loaded Grady on it. The doctor held the door as the outlaw was carried out of the office and he waited for a moment before following them. 'I hope you've got all the information you require Captain Hart. I doubt if that outlaw will make it through the night. But I'll do what I have to do though…' he left the sentence in mid-air and shaking his head strode quickly off to catch up with the stretcher-bearers.

'You did well, son, bringing Grady in alive. We've got enough information now to make a move on the gang who slaughtered Leeward and the Circle E.'

'But we can't put everything back the way it used to be,' John Gideon said softly, taking Captain Tom Evans's watch out of his pocket and looking from it to the older ranger. The cold expressionless eyes of the young man before him did not blink or register anything other than cold revenge. It seemed to Jack Hart that John Gideon Shaw was becoming capable of killing without compunction and perhaps enjoy doing it. The trouble with avenging angels was that they could lose their haloes. Jack Hart glanced at the saddle-bags which John Gideon said contained the retrieved stolen money and then across to the watch which the young man had put on the table. Returning to his seat, the ranger captain picked up the watch and pocketed it.

'I'll take this back to Tom Evans when I go visit him. I got a telegram saying he's making a recovery but that it'll take time.' His comment got no visual response from the young man.

Hart frowned and paused to think before taking the watch from his pocket and proffering it back to John Gideon.

'I've a better idea. You take the watch and return the money to Leeward. Captain Tom will be more than delighted to see you. Well, what do you think?' The cold expression on the young ranger's face did not lighten up.

'I think I should get back along the border to try to intercept one or other of the groups before they join up in San Credo. I 'specially want to meet up with the one named Wilson.'

Jack Hart had to agree that Shaw had a better chance with three or four of the outlaws than if he waited for them to get together into a larger group.

'Then you'll need some of this cash to play the part,' he said, pocketing the watch once more and pushing some of the money from the saddle-bags across the table towards the young ranger.

'Get some food and rest,' he said. 'Then you can be on your way again tomorrow.'

John Gideon agreed and went to find a wholesome meal and a comfortable bed. He would look in on Jack Hart before he left town.

The next day, unshaven and still dressed

in his dusty clothes, the young ranger collected his refreshed grulla, food and ammunition, and set off along the silent street. As he came level with the ranger's office, the door opened and Jack Hart stepped onto the boardwalk.

'Try and get some news back to me, John Gideon; it would help if we knew where they were aiming to strike next. But first and foremost get yourself back, d'you hear?'

'Will do, Jack. Tell Captain Evans I'm sure glad to hear his good news and tell him I hope to have some myself quite soon.'

'By the way, son, I got news this morning that the girl from the café in Leeward is safe. She's gone to visit relatives. Probably stay there I shouldn't wonder.'

The first Mexican town John Gideon rode into looked much like the last one where he had met Grady and his two companions – a store, a cantina and a few adobe buildings. He stayed only long enough to confirm that there were not, nor had there been, any gringos stopping over recently. He left the town as he had entered, without attracting attention, allowing his horse to set the pace. Once free of the town environs he picked up speed and covered quite a few miles before the trail led him into a rocky pass. Keeping a brisk pace, the horse and rider travelled on.

The next sign of habitation came as a surprise to the young rider as he rode out of the rocky canyon that had supplied him with a safe resting place for his night's stopover, and enough grass and fresh water for his grulla. He found himself travelling along a gently undulating tract of land. He stayed his mount and studied the landscape before him. The trail cut through a broad swathe of cultivated fields of vegetables on one side and ripening corn on the other. Ahead, down the road apiece, smoke rose wispily from an adobe building. To his right, clumps of fruit trees edged the tall corn. On his left, at the far side of the field, he spotted a group of people busy about their business as they bent over harvesting the crop of melons.

John Gideon nudged his grulla and his horse walked on in the direction of the house. Two of the workers in the melon field straightened up from their labours and, having watched him for a while, began to angle across to meet the rider, further up the trail. The other three workers stood watching, hands on their hips, glad of the chance to stand and rest. John Gideon could see that they were two women and a boy. The two crossing the field to meet him were a middle-aged Mexican and a youth. He watched them intently, his hands loose-hold of the reins. Suddenly with a shriek two small bodies hurtled from the cornfield on his right and their mingled cries – as the first one stumbled and the second pounced upon him – caused the grulla to rear, throwing John Gideon to the ground. Startled but unhurt, John Gideon got to his feet and, calming his grulla proceeded to dust himself down. The two children picked themselves up and ran shouting across the field towards the female Mexicans.

By this time, the approaching male workers had broken into a run and were near enough for Shaw to see that the younger of them carried a machete, which by the look of it, had been used for harvesting the melons that grew in abundance. John Gideon made no move to remount, but stood waiting for the Mexican farmers with his hat in his hand as a sign of respect.

The elder of the two rattled away in Spanish, pointing from the cornfield to the children, to the ranger, to the farmhouse. Stopping as abruptly as he started and seeing the ranger's puzzled expression, he pushed the younger Mexican towards the stranger with a curt command.

'*Señor, my padre,* he say sorry. Children bad.' The elder Mexican interrupted.

'My *padre* he says you come to *casa* to clean up. It is siesta soon. Time to rest.'

'Tell your father thank you. I hope the children are not hurt.'

'No worry about them. Too much they play,' the young one retorted.

Turning, he translated for his father and the three set off along the road after the young Mexican had hailed the others working in the field.

'Have there been any other gringo riders passing by here recently?' John Gideon asked as they strolled along the road to allow the other workers to catch up with them. The older Mexican looked to the younger one.

'No, *señor,* no gringos round here,' the young Mexican replied after conferring with his father. The chatter of women's voices raised in gentle scolding sent the older Mexican into a tirade which resulted in the two children scurrying behind the older woman where they grabbed her skirts and vainly tried to pull her back into the field. The two women turned their faces to John Gideon and smilingly they addressed him in Spanish which the younger Mexican translated as their apologies for the children's behaviour. The women looked like mother and daughter. The girl was in her teens and was the image of the older woman. The boy with them nodded and, saying something to the girl, they both took the youngsters in hand and set off ahead of the group. It was evident to John Gideon that this was a complete working family of farmers.

'*Que pasa?*' the older woman asked, and John Gideon watched her face as the older Mexican told her what had happened. She turned to address the tall handsome gringo and smiled apologetically as the young Mexican conveyed her comments.

John Gideon smiled and bowed his head. 'Thank the kind *señora* for her words and tell her I am unhurt.'

'She is my *madre* and she says she will go on ahead and prepare some food and drink. She is honoured that you will join us.'

The young Mexican girl was waiting to usher John Gideon to a place at the long wooden table alongside the building. She bustled to and fro, in and out of the house, helping her mother with the cakes and lemonade, blushing shyly at the tall stranger's appreciative stare.

The young girl placed a glass of freshly made lemonade in front of John Gideon before taking her place at the table and her mother pointed to the cakes and motioned for him to take one, which he did with a smile.

Once the family were all seated, the young Mexican silenced the younger ones and turned to John Gideon. 'Now we are all here, Papa tell me to say I am Mano,' he said, stabbing his chest with his thumb. 'And this is my *padre*, Pepe–'

'Pepe Lamas,' his father interrupted. 'Lamas. Pepe Lamas.' He smiled at their visitor.

'Señor Lamas.' The young ranger bowed his head. 'Señora Lamas.' He acknowledged the older woman. Catching the eye of the young girl John Gideon smiled. 'Señorita Lamas–'

'You must not give her big head,' Mano interrupted with a laugh. 'She is just Rosa, my sister, and this one is my brother,

Raoul.' The youngster nodded formally. '*Señor*, and you are…?'

'I am John Gideon Shaw and I am looking for some gringos who have come over the border.'

Pepe listened while his son translated the ranger's words.

'*Señor*, why you look for gringos?' Mano asked. 'They are *bandidos*?'

The older children understood English but the parents struggled most times. Even so, the whole family turned their eyes towards their visitor and even the little ones sat waiting quietly.

John Gideon sipped his fruit drink. The strong lemon bit the back of his throat.

'Yes, *si*,' was all he said, and proceeded to eat his cake.

The whole family began to speak at once, in their own tongue. Mano listened to each member. His parents showed the most concern. His father wanted to know if the gringo *bandidos* were heading their way. The family quietened again as Mano put the question to John Gideon.

'I don't think so,' the ranger replied. 'It's towns they stay in while they have money to spend. They ain't been seen in the last town I passed through which suggests they're not hereabouts.'

'Ah, *si*. *Gracias*, Señor Shaw.'

Mano informed his family that they were in no immediate danger and the talk moved on from bandits to farming. It appeared that John Gideon was riding through a wide stretch of farming land between two border towns. Local Mexican farmers sold their harvested crops to the towns in the area. The conversation turned to the question of the nearest town and Mano told the young ranger that that would be Acuna, lying five miles to the north-east.

Perhaps the men John Gideon sought would be there. Rested and refreshed, the young stranger thanked the family for their hospitality and left.

The big grulla was frisky and fresh and did

not need any encouragement to stride out. About two miles further on, three riders rode into view. If they were members of Embrel's gang he wanted to be ready. The young ranger slowed his mount and loosed his Navy Colt in its holster as the three riders headed towards him. However, as they got closer he could see they were Mexicans. Unkempt and well armed, they all carried Colts and saddle guns. They spread across his path, barring his way.

'Ah, Señor Gringo,' the oldest member addressed him, his smile showing his tobacco-stained teeth. 'You are lost, no?'

'I'm not lost, no.'

The Mexican's smile vanished at the answer to his question. He turned to each of his companions. 'He is not lost. You have money, Señor Gringo?'

John Gideon nodded. 'I have money.'

'*Bueno*. That is good. To pass, you pay. All gringos pay.' His hand moved to rest near his Colt. His companions did likewise.

'Twenty dollar American.' The brown-stained teeth were shown again as he smiled.

John Gideon studied the three men, his eyes unflinching.

'For twenty dollar American, you do not die, gringo. This is very cheap, *si?*'

One minute the Mexican was in charge, speaking with confidence, the next he was looking at John Gideon's Navy Colt which appeared, as if from nowhere, to point at the belly of the Mexican leader.

'Step to one side or I'll kill you,' the ranger said, his finger tightening on the trigger. The Mexican raised his hands clear of his weapons. '*Señor,* I jest,' he said. The man on his left snatched at his gun. John Gideon's Navy Colt barked once. The bullet hit the Mexican in the shoulder. His gun fell from his fist as he tumbled backwards out of the saddle. The Mexican leader thought he saw a chance to draw his gun. The Navy Colt fired again, then again. Both Mexicans' hats lifted off their heads and their horses reared up. It took both men a while to gain control of their mounts. By the time they had, the young gringo had hightailed it down the trail. The two Mexicans cursed as they retrieved their hats before going to the aid of their *compadre* who sat groaning, holding his shoulder. His shirt was bloodstained, but on inspection, it was found that he had only suffered a flesh wound. They padded the injury with his dirty neckscarf before riding on. The three men knew they could have been left for dead. The gringo had been charitable.

Having put a safe distance between himself and the three Mexicans, John Gideon reined in his grulla and turned round to see whether they had decided to follow him. Perhaps he had taught them a lesson, he mused, as he replaced three spent shells in his Navy Colt, but he doubted if men like them ever learnt. The young ranger frowned. They were riding on towards the farm he had left earlier. He recalled the gentle ways of the Lamas family and patting the big grulla's neck he rode slowly forward, back to where he had come from.

SEVEN

The three Mexicans rode into view of the Lamas family as they left the *casa* to return to the field. They stopped and waited for the riders to approach the farmhouse. One of them rode clumsily with one hand clutching at a bloodstained shoulder. The farmer whispered to young Raoul, who grabbed the hands of the two youngest and moved to the edge of the little group. The three riders halted their horses outside the *casa* and to the leader's command, one of them dismounted to assist the injured rider to climb down from his horse. Mano stepped forward to greet them.

'You need help, *señors?*' he asked.

'When we need help we will tell you,' snarled the leader, dismounting to assist his companion to seat the injured man at the table. While their attention was distracted, and at his father's silent signal, Raoul disappeared round the corner of the adobe building with the youngsters in tow. He would go to the predesignated place overlooking the *casa* and not return till his family signalled it was safe to do so. Señora Lamas gently eased her daughter behind her and mother and daughter backed away from direct confrontation with the riders.

The leader straightened up and stepped away from the table to face the farmer and his family. What he saw did not impress him as threatening and his manner eased as he studied the women, his eyes lingering on the young girl, Rosa.

'We were attacked by a gringo. We chased him off but he managed to shoot Pancho. Now we need to bathe the wound and ask some questions.'

Señora Lamas stepped forward with a forced smile. 'We will help you. I will get you some refreshment while you talk with my husband. Come, Rosa.' She turned and pushed her daughter ahead of her into the house. The gang leader made to follow them to find his way barred by Mano who said, 'You stay, talk with my *padre*.'

The leader pulled his gun and poked it in Mano's ribs. 'No, you stay here. First I talk with the ladies.' Mano glanced behind the leader to see that his companions had drawn their guns and that they were pointing at himself and his father.

'You and your *padre* can talk all you want to my *compadres*.'

'Rico. Pancho. Listen carefully to what they have to say about the gringo who must have passed this way.'

Mano was hauled back to join his father and dumped on a chair.

'Rico,' the leader continued, 'make sure I am not disturbed. If they try to leave the table shoot them. I will go and talk to the ladies.'

Mano started to rise to his feet and Pancho's gun exploded, the bullet drilling a deep furrow along the table.

'The next one will kill you, *amigo*,' the wounded man said. Mano froze and his father told him to think of the family and to sit still. The young Mexican reluctantly did as he was bidden. The gang leader laughed, took off his sombrero and entered the house.

At the sharp retort of gunfire ahead, John Gideon Shaw instinctively pulled his grulla off the trail and slowed down to a walk. From the shelter of the bordering fruit trees he continued his journey at a slower pace having pulled his Winchester from his saddle scabbard. As he neared the adobe farmhouse, he could make out Pepe Lamas and Mano, who were seated stiffly at the table with two of the riders he had earlier encountered. There was no sign of the other member of the trio nor the rest of the Lamas family. John Gideon dismounted and, leaving his grulla tied to a tree, made his way stealthily on foot towards the farmhouse. Nearing the *casa*, he stopped behind a bank of rocks. From this vantage point he could see that Pepe and Mano were being held at gunpoint. One of the seated bandits got to his feet and with his head still turned towards the farmer, began to move towards the house. The young ranger jacked a bullet into the breech of the Winchester and took careful aim at the moving target.

From the house, a woman's cry rent the air and John Gideon tightened the pressure on the trigger of his rifle. Halted in mid-stride Rico spun round and fell back, blood oozing from the side of his neck. The sound of the shot had not finished echoing out when John Gideon fired again. The seated Pancho looked in disbelief at his companion, but before he could react, his world blacked out as a .30 slug hit him in his chest.

Mano sprang to his feet, ran forward and snatched the gun from the seated, dead Mexican. He kicked Rico's gun over to his father and froze on the spot at the sound of his mother's voice, 'Please, *señor*, leave her alone.'

The sound of a slap and a cry of anguish sent him bounding over to the house with his father in quick pursuit.

'Mano, Pepe,' she gasped, as she collapsed against the wall, with blood running from her mouth. Young Rosa lay on the floor. The bandit leader was lying on top of her, one hand holding her struggling frame, the other tearing at her clothing.

'*Bastardo*,' Mano shouted, aiming a kick at the heaving frame of the Mexican who seemed, until then, oblivious to his presence. The gunman turned and looked up to see Mano standing over him with a .45 in his hands. The Mexican bandit paled and scrambled forward over the protesting girl to grab his own gun which was lying on the floor just beyond his reach, where he had placed it at the beginning of his struggle with the girl. The gun in Mano's hand went off.

The bullet drilled into the gunman's neck at the base of his skull. As he fell sideways, Rosa's muffled screams were released and she rolled clear to scramble towards her mother's waiting arms. Mano pumped the gun again and again each bullet jerking the inert body of his sister's assailant. Pepe Lamas guided his wife and daughter outside and sent them off to get Raoul and the little ones before returning to find Mano shouting threats and firing the now empty gun, again and again.

'Mano,' his father called sternly. The young man continued to scream abuse at the bullet-riddled body of the dead bandit, deriding him as the evil one who had beaten his mother and tried to rape his sister.

'Mano.' His father raised his voice. 'It is time to stop. We must put these bad men away before your mother returns with Raoul and the children.'

His father's even tone of authority poured over the young boy's anger and Mano nodded his agreement.

'Rosa?' he asked.

'Your mother says she will be fine,' his father answered their unspoken fears.

The sound of hoofbeats pounding along brought Mano and his father back to a state of alert. What if the *bandidos* had other companions? Holding their breath the two farmers watched from the window as the rider came into view. They were relieved to see John Gideon Shaw dismounting with his Winchester clutched in his hand. Mano threw down the empty gun when he recognized the ranger. 'Señor Shaw, it was you who fired the shots. It was you who saved us. *Gracias,* my friend.'

Greetings and information exchanged, the ranger, the farmer and his eldest son set to to dispose of the bodies. They buried them in a hastily prepared grave, some distance away from the farm.

By the time they had completed their task, Señora Lamas, young Rosa, Raoul and the little ones had returned to the *casa* and a start had been made to clean away any remaining evidence of the presence of the violent bandits and their subsequent deaths. The women brushed and scrubbed and young Raoul tended to the three newly acquired horses that now belonged to the Lamas family. With regular care and good food they would become a welcome addition to the farm.

When all was done, the Lamas family invited the ranger once more to join them for a meal. Afterwards, with Mano acting as interpreter, John Gideon told the family how he had met the three bandits and the outcome of that meeting. He apologized, blaming himself for stirring up a hornet's nest.

'No,' said Pepe. *'Hombres muchos malos.'* The Mexican farmer went on to thank John Gideon formally for saving their lives and added that he was glad that the ranger was not hunting him or his family and that they must find a way to repay him for what he had done.

John Gideon brushed aside their thanks and stood up to say his goodbyes.

'I must go. I have much to do,' he explained, adding, 'It would be as well to keep the guns of the dead bandits hidden away in a safe place, just in case. You never know when you may need them.' He waited while Mano interpreted his suggestion. The farmer nodded in agreement and Mano spoke to his father some more. Pepe Lamas glanced worriedly towards the ranger then sighed and nodded.

'What have you told your father? I don't want to alarm him,' John Gideon said.

'No, no, Señor Shaw. I will explain. I, Mano Lamas, will go with you. My father agrees. I help you. You speak Spanish – not good. I speak like gringo – very good. I help you find bad gringos, here in Mexico. This way my family say thank you.'

Mano finished with a flourish of his arms that took in all the family and waited with baited breath. John Gideon Shaw swept his gaze over the faces of the expectant family.

'You could end up dead, young Mano, tell your father that.'

Mano shook his head impatiently. 'Only he will want to know who I die with. Will I tell him you are a bad gringo, a good man, a bounty hunter, a lawman? This he would like to know.'

John Gideon smiled at the determined face jutting towards him. Pulling out his ranger's badge he gave it to Mano to show to his father. Pepe Lamas nodded with respect and the youngsters gasped, wide-eyed as their father explained what the ranger's badge stood for. The keepers of law and order were well known along the borders of Texas and Mexico.

Inspection complete and approval granted, John Gideon took the badge and returned it to his pocket. 'Well, young friend, we really must be going. Where's your horse?'

'I have it. Wait here,' Mano shouted as he darted off to return, a while later, with the best of the three horses the bandits had owned. Raoul helped him pack what he needed, his mother provided enough food for both riders and his father, Pepe, presented Mano with one of the rifles that had belonged to the bandits and the Colt .45 he had used to kill the Mexican leader.

John Gideon meanwhile had mounted his grulla and ridden off apace, leaving the young Mexican to make his final private farewells. Finally, Mano climbed aboard the horse and with a loud *'Adios,'* jammed his booted heels into the side of the beast and hastened to catch up with John Gideon Shaw.

'Wait, *señor,'* he called. 'I take you a better way to Acuna.' Catching up with the ranger the two riders turned to wave goodbye to the family. John Gideon tipped his hat to the young Rosa, who watched shyly before waving with growing enthusiasm as her brother and the handsome ranger disappeared into the swathe of corn. John Gideon pulled his grulla back to allow Mano to lead and permitted himself a secret smile as he straightened back in the saddle. He knew then that he had to return Mano alive to his family if only as an excuse to see the farmer's daughter once again.

EIGHT

'Well, Señor John Gideon, what do you think of Acuna?' Mano Lamas spread out his hands. 'It is big, no?' The young ranger sat his horse and took in the bustling town that was before him. Even as he glanced round at the mixture of wood and adobe business buildings and family dwellings, gunfire rang out. Mano straightened to pull at the gun tied to his waist, but John Gideon snapped for him to leave it where it was.

'On second thoughts,' he urged, 'get that gun out of sight. Put it in your saddle-bag. I don't want any trouble.' It did not take him long to spot the source of the outburst at the far end of the town. The area around the disturbance quickly became deserted as passers-by scattered for safety leaving a young, drunken cowboy firing his weapon

115

randomly into the air.

An unfortunate Mexican tried to scurry behind him but the drunk turned on his heels and, grabbing the man by the shirt neck, swung him into the dirt road. Again the shots rang out as the Mexican hopped about trying to dodge the bullets which were bouncing around his feet. From a safe distance the locals watched as the poor victim did a kind of dance till the gun became silent – the hammer finally coming down on an empty chamber. The drunk swayed as he inspected and then holstered his spent .45 before staggering off down the street to vanish into a nearby cantina signalling that the town could, for the moment, return to normal.

'That's why I don't want you carrying a gun, Mano. If any trouble starts, I'll sort it out, d'you hear? Come on.'

Shaw heeled the big grulla forward into the main street with a thoughtful Mano riding a pace or two behind. Perhaps the ranger was right. He could shoot a pistol but he was no *pistolero*.

The two rode slowly through the crowded thoroughfare where, John Gideon was surprised to find, there were as many Americans as there were Mexicans.

Although it was not Mano's first visit to Acuna he had never stayed longer than his father's farm business had warranted. It looked bigger every time he visited.

'My father says the best stable is at the other side of Acuna,' he volunteered, catching up with John Gideon.

'Good,' the ranger replied. 'Did he also tell you where is the best place to stay?'

Mano's face became crestfallen. 'We do not stay in Acuna, *señor*, but if you mention my father's name, everybody knows Pepe Lamas.'

'Everybody?' queried John Gideon playfully.

'Most everybody, I think,' was the subdued reply.

As they passed a saloon at the far end of town, a body came hurling out of the swing doors and landed near the grulla's feet. The big horse snorted and shied away, kicking out at its antagonist who rolled away and frantically scrambled to his feet. Mano pulled his horse deftly to one side as John Gideon calmed his grulla and turned him about to face the saloon.

The swing doors opened again and a red-faced man stomped on to the boardwalk. He paused for a second till his eyes fixed on the young drunk unsteadily dusting himself down in the street.

'Hey, fool,' he challenged. 'If you can't hold your liquor, stay on milk.'

The young cowboy lurched forward. 'I'll show you who's a fool,' he retorted, reaching for his gun.

His draw was quick, even though he was drunk, but the trigger clicked on an empty chamber.

He laughed with derision as the red-faced man drew his gun and fired. The bullet hit him in the chest and the young cowboy staggered backward on his heels, struggling to maintain his balance. His ears filled with the sound of rushing winds and, shaking his head, he spread his feet in an attempt to steady himself. Shakily he lifted his gun and tightened his finger on the trigger but again it clicked dully on an empty chamber. Then his young legs buckled and he pitched forward to lay still.

The gunman on the saloon boardwalk, replaced his pistol and looked about him. A silent crowd stared back at him.

'I didn't know his gun was empty,' he exclaimed, shaking his head. 'I didn't know.'

'When Wilson finds out what has happened, he won't be happy about it.'

The big man looked about him, seeking out the speaker, but nobody spoke. His eyes fell on John Gideon. 'You saw what happened, mister. You saw him draw first. You can tell them what I said is true.'

The dead cowboy was obviously the one they had seen earlier shooting at the Mexican, but the young ranger was not prepared to get involved. John Gideon shook his head. 'I'm sorry. I don't know what happened,' he retorted, and nudged his horse round to continue down the road towards the town livery. Mano looked back to see the big man re-enter the saloon and wondered why John Gideon had refused the man's request for help. He shook his head. 'Gringos,' he muttered and for a split second wondered if he had done the right thing riding here with John Gideon.

Almost immediately, the thought was thrust from his mind. How could he be so disloyal to this man who had saved the lives and honour of his family? He thought of his sister, Rosa, and what would have happened if the ranger had not killed the two *bandidos,* giving him the chance to kill his sister's abuser. He blessed himself as the livery stable came into view.

Their horses were duly stabled and John Gideon paid for a week's livery. Taking their travelling bags and guns they sought out a decent lodging that Mano knew of in the Mexican quarter. It was clean and cheap and the food was ample.

Later, John Gideon decided to take a walk round the town. Nearing the saloon, where the drunken cowboy had been shot, he saw that a crowd of townsfolk and cowpokes had begun to gather. He approached the crowd and heard a man's raised voice.

'I'm not a gunfighter. I'll fist fight you.' There was a frightened ring to the challenge. With the advantage of height, John Gideon could see what the commotion was about from the back of the crowd. Two men faced each other. The one Shaw recognized as the big man who had gunned down the young drunk in the street, had his saddlebags and slicker tossed over his shoulder, ready to leave town in a hurry. Facing him stood a smaller, slimmer man, about five foot eight tall and of wiry build. Round his waist was a well-worn gun belt and the holster was tied down by a leather cord.

'I don't fist fight,' was the grim reply. 'You're a big man. This here .45 brings you down to my size. Now put down that slicker and bag.' His cold grey eyes did not blink and his slim fingers caressed the Colt .45.

The big man looked about him with fear etched on his face. 'I didn't mean to kill him,' he dry-mouthed, as his eyes searched the faces around him.

He spotted the tall frame of John Gideon Shaw at the back of the crowd, 'Hey you, mister. You saw it. Tell him. Tell him he drew first. I didn't know his gun was empty.'

The little gunman's eyes flickered over in the direction of John Gideon Shaw for a second before returning to the big man.

'Bradshaw, I'll give you a chance. I'll empty my gun and leave one bullet in it.' So saying, he ejected the bullets from his .45 before replacing one bullet. 'Now, Bradshaw, I'll count to ten.'

The big man looked about him as the people around him moved clear, not wanting to be caught by any stray bullet. At the count of five Bradshaw dropped his bag and slicker and his big hands clenched and opened nervously. Not waiting for the count to finish, he moved, surprisingly quickly for such a big man, and stepping to one side, snatched at the gun at his side. The little gunman moved in unison. His gun was up and lined, making Bradshaw's draw look slow and cumbersome in comparison. The big man thought he had beaten him to the draw and his finger began to tighten on the trigger as the little gunman's .45 exploded. The bullet hit Bradshaw in the chest. His gun fell from his grip and he clutched at his chest. His fingers pulled at his shirt as the red liquid oozed through it. The big man's eyes dulled and he fell forward, twitched and lay still. The little gunman opened his .45 and punched out the empty casing. Then he filled the empty chambers before replacing the gun to rest at his side.

'Well done, Wilson.'

Two men stepped forward, one of them shouting his praises as they patted him on the back. The man, Wilson, laughed as he took the compliment. He looked up and saw the tall man staring at him from the back of the crowd. John Gideon Shaw stood mesmerized, staring at the man called Wilson. What was it Grady had said? It was Wilson who had dragged Sam to his death. Is this the same Wilson? Is he the man?

'Have you anything to say, stranger?' Wilson challenged, as he met the stare of the young ranger.

John Gideon shook his head. 'Reckon he got what he deserved,' he commented laconically.

The man Wilson nodded his head. 'You can say that again,' he concluded, turning his attention back his two companions.

Once again the crowd drifted away leaving the still form of Bradshaw to be tended to by a Mexican in a black suit. He was the town's undertaker. Expertly and diligently he searched the dead man's pockets before signalling to helpers to move the body. Any money found would pay for the funeral of the deceased. In a matter of minutes the area was cleared and the town went about its business as if nothing untoward had occurred.

There was no law in the town of Acuna only the *Federales*, who came and went when it suited them. As long as the gringos killed only themselves and their Mexican *compadres* they left things alone. They were only interested in their own needs and to make sure that nothing interfered with them.

John Gideon Shaw followed Wilson and his two friends into the saloon. Seeming to ignore them, he bought himself a drink and sat down. A young Mexican lad was mopping up and stopping occasionally to collect a glass or two and wipe spills from table tops. Catching his eye, John Gideon signalled him over. The proffered coin caught the boy's interest and he listened eagerly while the gringo talked. He wiped the table energetically before resuming his mopping and the ranger finished his drink and left the saloon having noted that Wilson and his two companions were well settled in the far corner at the end of the bar.

John Gideon went back to his lodging where Mano was waiting for him. Quickly he told him that Wilson and his two companions were the men he was after and explained his plan before the two made their way outside. Leaving Mano to follow, John Gideon crossed the road and entered the saloon and casually nodded to the waiting young Mexican who left the building in search of Mano.

Getting himself a drink, the young ranger settled himself at a table and waited for Mano to enter. He did not have to wait long. His young friend slid into the saloon with his head down over his mop. Working his way around the room he eventually arrived at John Gideon's side. As he slowly swabbed the floor around the table, John Gideon waited till the young Mexican was facing directly opposite the table where the three rowdy gringos were and then he gripped his young friend by the knee. Without flinching, Mano stopped in his tracks and, taking a wet rag from his belt he began to wipe down the table top. The young ranger identified the three raiders as he raised his glass to his lips. Raising his head from his labour Mano could not mistake the noisy trio. He nodded and moved to position himself with his back to them.

'The short skinny one is Wilson. Go see what you can find out. I'll keep the barman busy,' John Gideon said, before purposely dropping his glass and spilling the remains of his beer on the table. Pushing himself from the chair he feigned a grab at Mano. 'You clumsy idiot. Get away from me,' he stormed, as he made his way to the bar. The Mexican boy sidled away to do as he was bid. *En route* he was pushed about and jeered at by the cowpokes who mistook him for the swamper. He circled the saloon and, keeping his head down, eventually found himself by Wilson's group, where his presence was ignored. He mopped the floor and wiped the bar and fiddled with the glasses long enough to get the gist of conversation before making his way back across the room to mop once more near to the ranger's table. John Gideon had got himself another beer and was grumbling beneath his breath as the young Mexican approached.

'Hey you, get this table cleaned up,' he growled to Mano.

'*Si, señor,*' Mano said, as he busied himself at the task. Wiping the table, he leant over to whisper through gritted teeth, 'The skinny man very angry. He say Keely was a fool to get hisself killed. He say Embrel will be mad as hell.'

'Embrel, are you sure he said Embrel?'

'*Si, señor,* Embrel – mad as hell.'

'Hop it,' John Gideon urged, as he stood up and strode to the bar to replenish his drink. Through the bar mirror he watched as Mano finished wiping the table top before mopping his way to the swing doors and finally disappearing through them to be replaced by the other young Mexican who took up the job where Mano had left off.

John Gideon stood at the bar and slowly sipped at his drink.

NINE

The young Mexican made his way back to the lodgings to sit and wait for John Gideon. It had all gone as his friend had predicted, but Mano had half hoped that he would have been needed in a shootout with the bad gringos. He sighed as he dragged a chair over to the window and straddled it so that he could watch the goings on in the street below while he waited for John Gideon to return.

In the saloon, John Gideon was taking his time moving away from the bar. He sipped at his beer and grunted approvingly as he turned sideways to find Wilson, who was leaning on the far end of the counter, eyeing him with a cold curiosity.

'That was some shooting out there,' the tall ranger said, waving his glass in salute.

'You gave him every chance.'

Wilson's expression did not alter. 'Yeah, it was and I did,' he retorted, before standing up straight and adding, 'Truth is stranger, I thought you was with him.'

'Nope,' John Gideon replied calmly, taking time to sip at his drink, 'I arrived just as the big fella shot the young cowboy down. He said he didn't know your friend's gun was empty, but he did. Just drew anyway and shot him. I reckon he got what he deserved.'

Wilson allowed a satisfied smirk to cross his lips as he gripped the neck of the whiskey bottle the barkeep had put on the counter.

'I'd buy you a drink,' John Gideon continued, 'but my funds are low.'

Wilson tossed a coin on to the bar. 'Let me buy you one. Are you on your own?'

The young ranger nodded. 'Yes,' he replied, 'and thanks.' With that he emptied his glass and the barman gave him a refill.

'Join us if you want to,' Wilson said as he moved away.

'P'raps I will, later. Thanks for the drink.'

Wilson nodded and returned to his table.

'What's up with the stranger?' Nolan asked him.

'Just said I did a good job on Bradshaw. Perhaps we could use him. We're a man short without Keely.'

Nolan studied the tall man by the bar and added. 'Perhaps we could. What do you think Smithy?'

Smith looked at John Gideon and said, 'I'll go along with whatever you two think.'

Wilson mentioned the fact that the tall stranger had a money problem. 'I'll talk with him later,' he concluded and watched the tall stranger finish his drink and leave the bar.

John Gideon was met by an eager Mano as he entered the lodging-room.

'Did I do well, Señor Shaw? Have you killed the bad gringos?' the young Mexican asked excitedly.

'Whoa, one thing at a time. Yes, Mano, you did well and no, I am still working on my plan for the bad gringos. After I parley with

Wilson this evening I'll have an important job for you. I'll need you to deliver a note, containing my report, to the Texas Rangers' Headquarters in Austin. Do you think you can do that?' Mano stood mouth agape listening intently before nodding slowly.

'I take it that's a yes,' John Gideon smiled. 'For now, we should both take a rest 'cos we'll need all our energy later on.' Stretching himself on one of the beds, Shaw placed his hat over his face and folded his arms in repose. Mano stifled his excitement and, taking the pillow from the other bed, he tossed it on the floor against the door. He lowered himself to the ground and sat cross-legged with his back against the door and cat-napped till the sky darkened and his ranger friend stirred himself and woke.

Mano brought a tray of food up to the room and after a quick meal John Gideon was set for a meeting with Wilson's gang. He paused at the door before leaving.

'Stay here, Mano. If I don't come back, don't come asking after me. Just make your way back home. Do you understand?'

Mano stopped chewing and nodded. Whatever danger his ranger friend faced, Mano Lamas would stand by him. He would be there waiting to carry his message to the head ranger in Austin, Texas and while he waited Mano decided he would pray – like he had never prayed before.

John Gideon Shaw paused momentarily in the doorway of the saloon, to seek out the table where Wilson sat with Smith and Nolan, before heading their way.

'Evening, gentlemen,' he said and stood waiting to be asked to sit with them. The invite came from Wilson.

'Grab a chair,' he said, tossing money to Smith. 'Get the stranger a drink and get another round for us.'

'That's mighty kind of you,' John Gideon said settling himself on the spare chair next to Wilson. 'And the name's Shaw.'

He decided to continue with his pose as a penniless drifter and hoped that Wilson might take a shine to his company and perhaps let drop some more information about Embrel and the gang's activities. As a precaution, he had left his money in his lodgings. It would not do for any of them to find out he had any. As far as Wilson knew, he was broke and it suited Shaw to let him go on thinking that.

Wilson introduced the tall young ranger to Nolan who nodded and identified himself.

Smith came back with the drinks, and wiped his hand on his trousers before shaking hands.

'Wilson said you might be interested in riding out with us,' he said.

'Well, that would depend on what kind of work you'd want me to do,' Shaw said.

Smith laughed. 'Work!' he exclaimed.

Nolan nudged Smith's arm as he sat down. 'Leave it,' he hissed.

Smith turned to Nolan. 'He's got to know what we do,' he said. Wilson told both of them to shut up and they did.

'Can you use that?' Wilson said, pointing to the ranger's Navy Colt.

'If I have to. Why?' was Shaw's studied reply.

'In the kind of work we do, you'll not get far if you're shy of using it,' Wilson replied.

'Shy's not a word I'd use to describe you,' John Gideon said. 'I've seen what you can do with a gun.'

Wilson laughed drily. 'I can use mine if I have to. It's a well-paid job but it's dangerous most times and not what one would call law-abiding.'

The young ranger pursed his lips as he turned his glass slowly round, pretending to give the offer consideration.

'How many of you are there? Will it be just us four?'

He waited for Wilson's reply.

'There's ten of us, altogether, when we're working. We raid a town, get what we want and ride on out. We cross the border into Mexico, spend what we have on drink, women and whatever – till the money runs out – then we meet up again and plan another raid.'

John Gideon looked about the saloon before asking, 'Where is the rest of your gang?'

Wilson laughed. 'They're not here. We split up after a raid. We have a month apart then meet up again. The boss always has a town picked out for us to raid. It's that easy. All you have to do is follow orders and if necessary use your gun. If that answers all your questions it's time for you to come up with an answer. Are you in or out?'

'Sounds OK to me. I'm in.'

'Good choice. Means you get to live longer,' was Wilson's chilling reply.

Shaw ignored the implication behind the remark. 'When do we meet up?' he asked.

'In about a week's time. We meet in San Credo, up north. That's when we find out our next job. The boss'll have the final say as to whether or not you're in or out. Don't see no reason why he'd turn you down, though. Go get your warbag and come back here. You'll lodge with us from now on. Now you're part of the gang.'

136

Emptying his glass and taking his leave, Shaw returned to where Mano was waiting. He told the young Mexican to prepare his horse and get ready to ride out while he wrote a note for the boy to take to Jack Hart at the Rangers' Headquarters in Austin.

Leaving the lodgings as surreptitiously as he could, Mano made his way to the stables and quietly and quickly set about saddling his horse for the journey. Leading it to an alley near the lodgings, he crept back to their room as John Gideon completed the letter for Jack Hart. It told of Shaw's forthcoming meeting with the raiders and of their usual plan of action and the possibility of intercepting Embrel's gang as they crossed the Mexican border in the near future.

'We are ready Señor Shaw – the horse and Mano Lamas,' the young Mexican said.

'Good,' smiled John Gideon. 'This letter is for Captain Jack Hart. Take it to the headquarters of the Texas Rangers in Austin, Texas.'

'I know, *señor.* I will not forget. I will not let you down. The word of a Lamas is–'

'Yes, yes, I don't doubt you, Mano, but you really must get going. The sooner you get there the sooner Jack Hart can put a plan in action.'

Mano blushed. *'Si, señor* ... and you ... what will I say you do if Jack Hart ask me?'

'Tell him to be careful who he aims at, it could be me. Now it's time for you to go. Here's money for your needs. Did you check the water bottle?'

'Do not worry for me, *Señor* Shaw, I am a Mexican. I know what is important to live,' the young boy said softly. 'And you, *señor,* you will remember what is important to live? *Si?'*

'Si, my good friend, and thank you. Now go – slow and careful till you're clear of town and then as fast as you can, to Austin. *Adios,* my *amigo* and *gracias* – *muchas gracias.'*

Mano slipped the letter and money inside his shirt and slid out of the room, the lodgings and the town. The young ranger collected his bedroll and strolled to the saloon to join Wilson's group.

A dusty, tired young Mexican boy rode into Austin. Mano had ridden his horse with sense and urgency. The stops had been sparse – only long enough to water his horse and rest it for a few minutes – before continuing at a steady pace to cover the long distance to Austin.

It was late in the afternoon when the boy found the Rangers' Headquarters and Jack Hart, who was now listening intently while Mano told him of how he and the family Lamas had become acquainted with John Gideon Shaw. The old ranger listened without interrupting and then, while the youngster tucked into the food the ranger captain had ordered for him, Jack Hart read the note. It contained John Gideon's account of witnessing Wilson shooting the man in Acuna and of him being asked to join the raiders. It told of his acceptance and that he and the three raiders would be in San Credo in a week's time. Jack Hart paused for thought. With the young Mexican riding in over two days that left the old ranger five days to get a plan ready.

Once the young boy had finished his meal, Jack thanked him for his help and made arrangements for him to stay overnight. A couple of hearty meals, a long soak in the tub and a good rest in a clean bed should put him right for his journey the following day back to his home and family.

Then Jack Hart ordered Biggs to get ready to take over while he went to call on Tom Evans at Leeward before going on to meet up with John Gideon in Acuna.

The days while he waited with Wilson dragged on for John Gideon Shaw. The raiders spent their money and time on drinks and women and the young ranger was included in most things. He had been accepted as a gang member.

Jack Hart left Austin by stagecoach. Time to take to the saddle when he had to. Nothing about him told of his profession. To others he was like any other ageing traveller. His guns were packed in his case with his clothes.

When Jack Hart arrived in Leeward, his first call was to the house of the town doctor to visit Captain Tom Evans, who was still there, being nursed back to good health. The old rancher gave his old friend Jack a full personal account of what had happened. While the ranger was there, Buck Beanpole called in. He was in town getting the Circle E supplies. Beanpole was glad to see Jack Hart and listened while the ranger told Captain Tom about John Gideon Shaw and what he had so far managed to accomplish and that he was, at present, in Acuna with three of the raiders.

'Did he find out who killed my Nell, the saloon girl?' Buck asked.

Jack Hart nodded, pulled out his notes and flicked through them till he came to the ones about what Grady had said.

'Grady said it was Embrel, the man in charge. He should be in San Credo now waiting for his men to meet up before riding out on another raid.'

'Where's this Grady now?' Buck Beanpole asked.

'He's dead. He died undergoing an operation to remove his leg.'

The ranch cook nodded. 'Best thing could happen to the likes of him. I'll leave you then to chat to the cap'n. See you later, boss.' Buck stood up to leave. 'Are you staying in town, Jack, or coming over to the Circle E?' he asked the ranger.

'Here for now. I've a few things to sort out, then I'm riding over to Acuna to keep an eye on young Shaw.'

Beanpole left, got his supplies and returned to the Circle E. Pat Wilkes, the ramrod, helped him unload.

'Jack Hart's in town. Said he was investigating the raid on the town. Gave a name to that murderin' coyote who killed my Nell.' Buck Beanpole stopped to swallow hard and compose himself before continuing. He went on to recount his visit with Captain Tom and his concern for the welfare of young John Gideon.

'I'll be glad when that boy comes back here,' Beanpole concluded. Pat Wilkes nodded in agreement.

'I'd better get on with some cooking,' Buck commented thickly and the ramrod left him to set about organizing the meal. Pat Wilkes made his way to the bunkhouse to inform the winter crew and joined them in a game of cards while they waited for Buck Beanpole's call to come and get it.

Buck Beanpole had not been his usual self since the raid and the death of Nell, his saloon woman, and his call to eat lacked his old banter and commentary. Pat Wilkes and the handful of men who made up the winter crew rose from the card game and made their way towards the cookhouse, where the food had already been laid out on the table.

Outside the cookhouse, stood a saddled

horse ready with saddle-bags, a rifle in the scabbard and a bedroll tied behind the cantle.

'Who's going riding, boss?' one of the crew asked Pat Wilkes. The ramrod was as puzzled by the questions as the man who had asked it.

'Don't know,' he replied, as he entered the cookhouse. Buck Beanpole wore his topcoat and hat. Pat Wilkes stopped in his tracks.

'Is that your horse outside, Buck?' Wilkes already knew the answer to his question by the look on the lanky cook's face but he waited for a reply.

'I'll be gone for a while, Pat. You can get your own grub ready till I get back.'

'You're going after the raiders, aren't you, Buck? Leave it to Jack Hart and John Gideon. You're no gunnie.' The tall frame of Buck Beanpole pushed past Pat Wilkes as the ramrod spoke.

'Now I know who killed my Nell and where I can find him, I can't leave it unsettled. I won't need a gun.' His huge fists closed tightly as he continued, 'Not if I can get close to him.'

The door closed behind Beanpole. The Circle E ramrod stood inside the cookhouse and listened as he heard the horse ride away. If Buck Beanpole got close to the saloon woman's killer Wilkes knew the Circle E cook would not need a gun but he had taken a rifle just in case.

TEN

Buck Beanpole had crossed the border into Mexico during the night. Down the trail apiece stood an adobe building. Smoke curling from the chimney told him somebody was about. The sun was climbing fast and the heat of the day began to envelop him. Buck reined in and removed his topcoat, tying it to the back of his saddle. He had ridden all night without a break, but was too all fired up to be tired. What he wanted most of all was information.

What did Jack Hart say the name of the town John Gideon was holed up in was?

Acuna! The name came to him as he jabbed the sides of his horse and made for the adobe building ahead of him. As he approached, the door opened and a man appeared in the doorway with a rifle firmly grasped in his hands. The lanky rider stayed his mount before raising his hands high and wide.

'Am I on the right trail for Acuna?' Beanpole asked.

'*Señor?*' The Mexican hefted his rifle to the level of the stranger's chest.

'I'm looking for Acuna,' Buck said. The Mexican stared blankly.

'ACUNA,' Beanpole emphasized the world as he mouthed it slowly.

'Ah, *señor*, Acuna!' The Mexican pointed off to his left, repeating, 'Acuna.'

Buck Beanpole nodded. '*Gracias*. How far?'

'*No comprendo*,' the man said.

'*Mañana?*' Beanpole asked. 'Will I get there tomorrow? *Mañana?*'

'Ah, no, *señor*,' the Mexican shook his head emphatically as he cradled his rifle to enable him to display all the fingers on one hand. '*Hoy! Cuatro … cinco horas!*' was his reply.

Buck took the answer to mean that he should be in Acuna before nightfall. He thanked the man and gathering up his reins he set off in the direction the Mexican had indicated.

Buck rode on at a steady gait, allowing the horse to set the pace. They stopped only once, when the heat of the day forced them to take shelter in the shade of some cotton-woods. The horse was fed and watered and Buck snatched forty winks after a light snack. Soon they were up and running again with a little more urgency demanded from the horse's stride.

It was near dusk when the weary horse and rider loped into town. Beanpole saw the livery stable ahead of him, the entrance faintly lit by a single oil lamp. Stiffly, he climbed down from his mount and pushed open the door. A Mexican hurried into view to stand looking up enquiringly at the tall skinny figure.

'Is this Acuna?' the lanky cook asked, massaging his aching back as he stretched himself even taller.

'*Si, señor,* this is Acuna,' the Mexican said,

his face breaking into a grin as the tall man delved into his pocket and fished out a handful of coins.

'D'you reckon you could take good care of my horse?' the lanky cook asked.

'*Si, Señor.* How long?'

Buck was relieved to find the Mexican could speak good English.

'I don't know yet,' Buck answered, as he handed the ostler a few dollars. 'Will that see you right for now?' he asked. The Mexican's smile widened as he pocketed the coins, '*Si, señor,* I look after him good.'

The Mexican accompanied Buck outside to collect the animal and waited while the lanky gringo unloaded his rifle and gear. Buck Beanpole walked slowly up the main street of what he saw to be a fair sized town, with an even mixture of Americans and Mexicans. It was obvious that the native Mexican population accepted the gringos who ambled along the sidewalk, frequenting the cafés and saloons. All were armed and carried guns of one sort or another.

Buck Beanpole himself did not go unnoticed. His tall gangling figure stood out, his arms burdened with his warbag and rifle. As his eyes searched for somewhere to stay, he noticed a sign which read: 'Americanos welcome. Good food. Clean beds'. He turned abruptly towards the sign.

It was then that a slightly built man stepped from the boardwalk into his path and the tired cook, hampered by his load, was unable to avoid the collision. The smaller man bounced off the big cook. Staggering sideways, he cursed under his breath as he regained his balance and before Buck Beanpole could apologize the man's hand had streaked down to his sidearm. The gun was drawn before Buck could blink. He heard the hammer on the gun go back and his automatic reaction was to lash out with his Winchester hitting the handgun. It clattered to the ground. The man swore out loud and bent down to recover the fallen weapon. Buck Beanpole swung and let go of his warbag and coat, catching the shorter man off balance again, impeding his vision and movement. The big cook gripped the man with his free hand, restraining his movements.

'Don't be so hasty,' he warned.

The struggling man straightened up as Buck Beanpole's carbine was jabbed firmly under his chin and levered. Head tilted back, he found himself looking into the tall man's eyes and saw a look that definitely did not encourage him to struggle further. He knew it would be best to agree to the tall man's request. This he did.

'OK, big man. We'll let it be.'

Beanpole released him and took a step backwards, keeping his Winchester pointing at the little man as he retrieved his handgun and holstered it.

'I'll see you again, big man. My name's Wilson,' he said, peering closely at the lanky cook. Beanpole's face was an impassive mask, despite the fact that the man before him had just identified himself as one of the raiders mentioned by Jack Hart. He said nothing though his finger momentarily tightened on the trigger.

'Go your way, Mr Wilson.' Beanpole's voice was low and even. The man Wilson nodded.

'Till we meet again,' he said, and turned to make his way to the nearest saloon. Buck watched him disappear inside before collecting his gear and entering the building that welcomed Americanos. He hoped it would be a less traumatic welcome than the one Wilson had given him.

Wilson entered the saloon. His two companions sat with John Gideon Shaw.

'You look as if you've just met a grizzly,' Smith said to him.

Wilson cursed as he answered, 'He was as tall as one.'

Nolan invited him to be seated. 'I'll get you a drink,' he said.

Smith wanted more details about who he had tangled with.

'I don't know,' was the reply, as Wilson

took his gun from its holster and checked it over.

Flicking it back into place he looked his partner in the face and grimaced. 'Whoever he was, he won't be as lucky next time.'

John Gideon did not show any interest at all in the incident. His thoughts were on Mano and whether or not he had managed to get through to Jack Hart.

The ranger captain, at that moment, was in Leeward, talking to Captain Tom Evans when Pat Wilkes came into the doctor's back room.

'Hello, Jack, I'm pleased you're here,' Wilkes said. Jack Hart wondered why the ramrod looked so worried and asked if everything was all right at the Circle E.

'It's Beanpole. He rode out last night. He's gone to find young Shaw and the man who killed Nell from the saloon.'

Hart cursed softly under his breath. 'I shouldn't have told him where John Gideon was. God knows what that crazy cook will do if his temper gets all fired up. He could mess up the whole business.' Jack Hart stood up to take his leave of his friend. 'I'll have to go and find him, Tom, hopefully before he gets there. I'll get a horse from the stables—'

'Take my roan,' Pat Wilkes interrupted, 'it'll get you wherever you want to go.'

The old ranger thanked the Circle E ramrod and stayed only long enough to collect the basic requirements for sustenance on his journey, which included his guns, and a jar of rubbing salve from the doctor's wife, to ease his aching joints. He climbed heavily into the saddle and settled himself before bidding his final farewell to the doctor and his wife.

'Mind you rub that salve in at the first twinge,' was the message echoing in his ears, as Jack Hart set off from Leeward. The big roan was eager to get going. Jack Hart's first port of call would be Acuna. He knew the way and pushed his mount hard and it responded to the ranger's demands just as Pat Wilkes said it would.

Buck Beanpole found the lodging-house clean and tidy. The notice outside lived up to its boast. Americans were well catered for – good food and plenty of steaming coffee and the bed was reasonably comfortable. The big cook slept soundly that night. His breakfast was plentiful the next morning and he was offered the services of a friendly lady but he declined. His first job was to find John Gideon Shaw.

He was standing at the door of the lodging-house, scanning the length of the main street, when he saw the big sweating roan, tied up outside the café on the opposite side of the road. It looked mighty like Pat Wilkes's horse. Had he followed him to Acuna? Buck crossed the street to check the brand. It was the ramrod's horse all right – the Circle E was marked on its rump – and it had been ridden hard. It must be Wilkes. Who else could it be? Beanpole walked into the café where a number of early risers were finishing their breakfast. Jack Hart finished his coffee and stood up.

Beanpole's lanky frame caught his eye as the cook walked towards him.

'Buck,' he said, striding forward to take the cook by his hand and elbow and propel him back out of the eating-house and out of earshot of the diners. Once on the street they hesitated as both of them spotted John Gideon Shaw heading towards them with three men.

It was Wilson who spotted Beanpole.

'Well, hello again stranger,' he said, stopping and moving away from his three companions, his hand resting on his hand-gun. 'Now let's see what you can do, big man.' He stooped in a crouch.

Young John Gideon stood still, momentarily caught off guard at seeing Jack Hart and Beanpole in the border town. He looked about expecting to see other rangers. He spotted the big roan belonging to Pat Wilkes but there was no sign of the ramrod.

Jack Hart looked at the lithe, confident stance of the challenger and knew he was looking at somebody who could use a gun.

Beanpole stood still waiting for Wilson to make a move. He spread his hands slowly away from his body. 'You've caught me without a gun,' he said.

Wilson's cold grey eyes took in his target and the older man alongside of him.

Nolan laughed. 'Don't let that stop yer,' he encouraged Wilson.

'Shut up,' Wilson retorted. 'Give him your gun,' he spat, signalling to Jack Hart.

The ranger shook his head. 'Nobody gets my gun,' he said.

'Leave it, Wilson. He has no gun.' It was John Gideon who spoke now. Wilson turned on his new acquaintance, the look of a killer in his eyes. 'Who told you to butt in?'

'He's not worth the trouble he could cause. He's not carrying a gun.' The young ranger tried to reason with Wilson.

'You're right.' Wilson said, suddenly turning to face Beanpole. His hand streaked down to his gun. Lifting it from its holster, in a clean, smooth movement, he put a bullet between the cook's feet. The lanky cook hopped like a cat on a griddle as the board beneath his feet splintered.

'That's a sample of what you can expect next time we meet, big man, with or without your gun,' Wilson said, as he holstered his weapon and pushed his way between Hart and Beanpole to enter the café, with Nolan and Smith close behind.

John Gideon hesitated momentarily behind them.

'See you in the stables, later,' he murmured, as he fumbled to remove his hat before following the others into the café.

Wilson called for a breakfast. He felt cockier now he had baited and belittled the big man. He had given him his come-uppance. He turned to John Gideon. 'Don't interfere with me again. That's something you'll need to remember if you are riding with us.' He banged the table.

'Hurry up with that food,' he called.

Outside, Buck Beanpole stood fuming, his big fists clenching and unclenching. Jack Hart had managed to restrain him and stop him following Wilson's crew into the eating-house.

'Pull yourself together Buck,' the ranger hissed, 'and come on. We'll get my horse to the stable and wait for young John Gideon to show up. There are plans to work out and I don't want you messing things up with your temper.' Cursing, Beanpole followed Jack Hart as he untied the animal and walked it to the town stable. There they waited. Buck Beanpole was detailed to see to the Circle E roan, leaving Jack Hart to converse with the town ostler.

John Gideon finished his breakfast and rose up from the table. 'I'll see you guys later.'

Wilson stared at him as he got up. 'Don't be sulking because I told you off. It's how I am. No hard feelings.'

The young ranger looked into the cold, grey eyes, 'I don't hold grudges,' he said, returning the cold look. 'I'm just going to check my horse for when we ride out.'

Wilson did not realize how near to death

he had been when he drew his Colt and placed the bullet between Buck Beanpole's feet. If it had hit the cook, John Gideon had been ready to kill all three of the gang.

The young ranger walked down to the stables after noticing the Circle E horse had gone from the tie rail. He pushed open the big door and glanced back down the street, before pulling it closed after him as he entered. Through the rotting wood of the door he could see the entrance to the eating-house he had just left. He watched patiently and after a while the door opened and Wilson, Smith and Nolan stepped into the street and set off in the direction of their lodging. Watching long enough to satisfy himself of their destination, John Gideon turned and stepped soft-footed further into the stable. He could hear voices in the back room. Recognizing two of them, he entered the room to find Jack Hart and Beanpole sitting with the ostler, coffee cups in their hands while the coffee pot steamed merrily on an old iron stove in the corner.

'*Hola, señor,*' The ostler made to rise.

'It's OK. Stay seated. I've just come to check my horse.'

The Mexican did not need any encouragement. '*Si, señor,*' and he sat down.

Jack Hart got up and tossed the coffee dregs on to the earth floor, then passed the cup to the Mexican.

'I'll make sure my horse has settled,' he said, laying his hand on Buck Beanpole's shoulder as the lanky cook made to rise. 'No, Buck, you stay here. Keep our friend talking. I won't be long.'

Jack Hart joined John Gideon at the stall and the two rangers walked out of earshot of the back room.

Buck Beanpole settled down, rolled himself a smoke and passed over his baccy and papers to the ostler.

'*Gracias,*' he smiled, as he took the makings. Buck Beanpole lit his cigarette and poured more coffee for himself and the Mexican. He knew he had come near to spoiling any plans John Gideon and Jack

Hart had made. He had better get this right, even if it cost him some of his stash of favourite tobacco.

In the stable, Jack Hart shook hands with his young ranger.

'I can't tell you how surprised I was to see you, Captain,' John Gideon said. 'How did you and Beanpole come to be here?'

Jack Hart proceeded to tell him what had happened, adding, 'Buck could have stormed in like a maverick in a thunderstorm and blown your cover. I'm partly to blame – telling him what I knew about the raiders. I should have figured he'd come looking for Wilson and use him to find Embrel.' John Gideon nodded in agreement, knowing the big cook and his feelings for Nell, the saloon girl.

'That was a close call there today. Buck was lucky Wilson did not shoot him. The man's a heartless killer,' he said.

'Has he mentioned when they will be riding out to meet Embrel?' Jack Hart asked.

'Nothing's definite, but it's getting near the time,' John Gideon replied, adding, 'There's going to be big trouble, Captain, if Wilson and Beanpole meet again. Wilson will push for a showdown just to show me how good he is with a gun.' Jack Hart nodded in agreement.

Buck Beanpole came from the back room complaining that he had supped enough coffee to sail a boat in and that no one smoked as fast as that there Mexican. He lowered his voice as he joined the rangers. 'It's good to see you, boy. What's happening?'

'John Gideon will stay close to the three raiders,' Jack Hart said, 'while you, Buck, you go and get your carbine and get back here, pronto. It's time we moved in and sorted out Wilson and his lot. Then we'll move on to San Credo for Embrel and the rest of his gang.'

Beanpole was back in a matter of minutes, his Winchester loaded and – as he put it – ready for bear.

The three men left the stable and made their way to the gang's lodging-house. As they came near, John Gideon went on alone. His orders were to take the three raiders by surprise and, once he had them under arrest, to open the door for Hart and Beanpole. The young ranger found Smith and Nolan packing their warbags. Wilson, who was cleaning his Colt .45, looked up as he entered.

'Did you check that horse of yours?' Shaw nodded. Wilson spun his gun, put it in its holster and drew it again. He was fast. He pointed the gun at John Gideon. 'Bang,' he said before replacing it with a coarse laugh. 'We're leaving soon as the others get here, but first I'm going to settle with that big galoot.'

John Gideon did not say anything. He glanced at Nolan and Smith, who were still packing up. Unlike Wilson, they were not wearing their gunbelts, which were draped over a chair.

John Gideon decided the time was right to

make his play.

'Get on your feet, Wilson. Let's see how good you really are with that gun of yours.'

The two men packing their bags stopped and looked at Shaw then Wilson.

Nolan laughed, 'Stop kidding, Shaw, and start packing. Wilson won't take any baiting.'

Wilson stood up facing John Gideon. The room went quiet.

'Shut up, Nolan. So our young friend thinks he can take me.' His grey eyes searched the ranger's face. Nolan reached for his gun-belt.

'Stay out of it, Nolan,' Wilson said, adding, 'Seems our young friend wants to prove something.' Wilson had now turned his attention back to John Gideon Shaw.

'I want to kill the man who dragged the Negro to his death at the Circle E.'

The answer startled Wilson temporarily, then his lips parted in a smirk. His hand streaked down. His gun fired but it was pointed at the floor as John Gideon's bullet hit him in the middle of his chest. His eyes stared. The head shook in disbelief, then the light faded from the cold grey eyes as he fell dead. Nolan automatically reached for his gunbelt. The ranger fanned his gun as he turned. The lead slug hit Nolan in the shoulder. He spun away from the chair, tumbling into the half-packed bag as he fell. He clutched at it in agony and pulled it on top of himself as he hit the floor. Smith raised his hands as the smoking gun pointed at him.

'Don't shoot,' he screeched. Fear had raised his voice an octave. The door burst open and Jack Hart was first into the room with Buck Beanpole close behind him. Both men sported their weapons. The ranger captain showed his relief as he saw the two men on the floor and the third raider with his hands raised in the air staring fearfully at the gun John Gideon had pointing at his heart.

Jack Hart checked the fallen gunmen. Wilson was dead. Nolan was moaning under the spillage of clothing from the half-packed bag. Jack Hart tossed the baggage clear and pulled the injured raider into the middle of the room, the blood from his wound marking a thin red trail.

'Well, young fella, you seem to have managed on your own,' Hart said, pointing to Wilson.

'Did you give him a chance?'

John Gideon nodded his answer.

Buck Beanpole pulled a wry face. 'It's more than any of this lot would have given you, son. Now then, Cap'n, where do we go from here?' he asked and waited for an answer.

'San Credo … to search for this Embrel fellow.'

Now that he saw that his life was not in any immediate danger, Smith regained some of his false bravado. 'You won't get Embrel,' he sniggered.

Before he could be stopped by either ranger, Buck Beanpole stepped forward swinging his Winchester and smashed it into the face of the raider. Smith gagged in agony as the butt of the gun ripped open his lips and knocked teeth from his gums. He fell over backwards. Beanpole stepped across the fallen body. One big hand clutched the now bloodied shirt front and he heaved the body upright. 'We'll get the murdering bastard and you'll tell us where he's holed up.'

The two rangers stood watching as Beanpole shook his hapless victim. Then the enraged cook jabbed Smith with his carbine.

'Don't,' Jack Hart's command barked out. Buck hesitated. 'Let's hear what he has to say.'

The bloodied raider was tossed across the room to land on top of Nolan, who lay still, blood running from his wounded shoulder. He groaned and swore as Smith landed on him.

At the sound of the profanities, something snapped in Buck Beanpole. He remembered what he and the Circle E crew had found on their return from the cattle drive – Tom Evans's bloodied body, the ripped and torn corpse of Sam and, later, the murdered remains of his woman, Nell. He leapt forward, kicked the struggling Smith flat on his back and jammed his Winchester under the raider's bloodied chin.

'Where in San Credo will this stinking dog, Embrel, be holed up? And exactly when are you due to meet him?'

The bloodied lips tried to form words as Smith stared at Beanpole. He could see the hatred in the big man's eyes. Smith heard Nolan moan as he was pulled to his feet by the two rangers. Smith tried to spit his contempt at Buck Beanpole, but his swollen lips were unable to propel the red spittle far. It dribbled down his front. The Winchester exploded and the .30 bullet took off the top of Smith's head. Beanpole stepped back and turned his attention to the other wounded raider. Nolan stood shocked, not believing what he had seen. He soiled his pants as Buck Beanpole jammed the rifle under his chin.

'Don't … please … don't. I didn't kill anybody. I wasn't at the town café when they killed the woman...'

John Gideon pushed Beanpole aside. 'Who killed the café owner?'

'It was Smith… I swear,' he whimpered, before babbling on again. 'I was there but I didn't kill her. I used her, but it was Smith shot her. He was as bad as Wilson and Embrel. Embrel is in San Credo. We join up in a couple of days' time.'

'That about tallies with what I know,' John Gideon confirmed.

'He'd better get himself cleaned up,' Jack Hart said. 'Buck and I'll go get the horses.' The ranger captain grimaced as he opened the door, and distracted John Gideon's vigilance just long enough for Buck Beanpole to let off another shot from his rifle. The bullet entered Nolan's ear, blowing his face apart. John Gideon looked at the unrepentant cook.

'You wouldn't have killed him, son. I did it

171

for what they've done. Now let's get after Embrel and take note John Gideon, when we find him, revenge is mine. You stay out of my way.'

John Gideon had never seen the Circle E cook so cold and vengeful. He recognized the deep embedded feelings of hatred and fury that he himself had to wrestle with daily since the mayhem at the Circle E. The young ranger knew that what he felt inside was not the law-abiding detachment that an upholder of law and justice should display. Embrel and his gang of raiders had turned Buck Beanpole and himself into avengers with personal scores to settle. His young shoulders slumped. He walked a fine line and no mistake.

Jack Hart broke the silence. 'He's right, John Gideon. What's done's done. We'll go to San Credo and take it from there. This Embrel will be a different breed of animal so don't let's go in bull-headed. We've been lucky so far. Seven of the ten raiders are dead. There's only three more left. But it ain't a time to get careless. Do you hear me, Beanpole?'

Buck Beanpole nodded and put his arm round the shoulders of John Gideon Shaw, 'I'm sorry for my outburst, son. You and Jack here got your job to do … lawful like.' He paused for a while to draw a deep breath, before continuing. 'Remember when you first joined the Circle E – you was a child brim full of vengeance. You don't need to go there again, John Gideon. I got vengeance enough for all of us.' His big arm released its bearlike grip from the young ranger's shoulders. 'Come on,' he said, let's finish the job we've started.'

John Gideon collected his belongings while Captain Jack Hart and the cook, Buck Beanpole, straightened the three bodies before going off to find the Mexican undertaker. A fistful of coins and no questions asked paid for the discreet removal of the three dead raiders who had supposedly killed each other in a shoot-out.

John Gideon took Hart and Beanpole to

the lodgings he had previously used when he had first entered Acuna. A clean up, a filling meal and a good night's rest would see the three rested and ready to tackle the final stage of their mission to San Credo.

ELEVEN

After resting up in Austin, having reported to Captain Jack Hart with the written information about Wilson and the other gang members, young Mano Lamas was eager to get back to his family across the Mexican border. He had such a tale to tell of his exploits with Señor Shaw and his meeting with the famous Texas Rangers. He spared neither himself nor his mount and nearing his family farm he urged his wearying horse on. As the sun rose high in the sultry sky, the trail threw up dust to coat the horse and rider in ghostly white.

Farmer Pepe Lamas, working close to the main adobe building, was alerted by his son, Raoul, to the plume of dust travelling from the distance along the trail which would lead to their abode.

Pepe frowned, it was unusual to see such a sight in the heat of the day. His eyes scanned the horizon looking for telltale signs of others in hot pursuit of the rider. There were none. Deciding it was still safer to be sure than sorry, Pepe instructed the rest of the family to stay indoors and he and Raoul prepared to meet adversity if any was forthcoming.

His wife and young Rosa, his daughter, took charge of the younger children and the family settled down to wait, with Pepe at the window and Raoul alongside the wall, at the ready to obey his father's commands.

As the dust-covered figure rode into closer proximity, Pepe Lamas let out a string of expletives which caused his wife to catch her breath and the youngsters to whimper at her reaction.

'*Madre de Dios,*' Pepe's voice and tone changed to one of surprise.

'*Quien es, Papa?*' Raoul's question went unanswered as his father rushed to the door and flung it open.

'Mano!' the farmer said, as he dashed outside to welcome his eldest son.

'Mano?' The family's concern changed from anxiety through disbelief to excitement and joy as they tumbled out of doors.

The young Mexican was dragged from the back of his sweating horse and slapped and patted as the Lamas family welcomed him home.

Eventually they became more organized. Rosa went for water so that Mano could refresh himself; Mama set to to prepare a meal. Raoul, having pointed out that the horse had been hard-run, took it off to be tended to; the youngest children scattered to find a place at the outdoor table and eventually all the family were seated and silence fell on the group as they settled down to eat. Once the meal was finished, Pepe called for *'Silencio'*, and nodding to Mano gave the signal for his eldest son to begin recounting his activities and deeds since he left the farm.

The family, including the little ones, sat

spellbound as he told his story, catching their breath with excitement from time to time, eyes widening as he recounted the shootings he had witnessed.

'Is Señor Shaw safe?' Mano's father enquired. The family swivelled their eyes from father to son.

Mano nodded. 'Yes, Señor Shaw is safe and now he waits for his friend the ranger captain, Jack Hart, to go and help him to kill the rest of the *bandidos.*'

His mother blessed herself and muttered a prayer for the safety of the Texas Ranger.

'Will you return to Acuna?' his brother, Raoul, wanted to know. Once again, the family waited for Mano's reply, especially his sister, Rosa, who sat wide-eyed in adoration. To his younger siblings, Mano was a hero. They already knew of his involvement in the shooting of the *bandidos* who had attacked their mother and sister. They wanted to know if their hero was staying home.

'I was told by the ranger captain to come back home.'

'But what of Señor John Gideon?' his sister asked, concern in her voice.

'He will be OK,' Mano assured her. 'He is a great *pistolero,* very fast. He has killed three men, *bandidos.* The ranger captain says he will make a great lawman. I hear him say so.'

'You should not have left him, Mano,' Rosa chided. 'He may still need you.'

Her father told her to be quiet. 'If Mano wishes to return to Acuna, he will, but only he can make that decision.'

The little ones begged him to stay and their hugs and tugs were very hard to ignore. However, that night, while his family slept, Mano saddled his mount and left his home, leaving a note for his father to say he would come back if John Gideon Shaw did not need him.

On his arrival at Acuna, Mano made enquiries at the lodging-house where he had stayed with the young ranger. He was very surprised to find that there were three Americanos sleeping there. He settled himself on the bench outside and waited for morning. When the three Americanos arose, and Mano ventured inside to see who they were, he recognized John Gideon and Jack Hart, but not the stranger, who was introduced to him as Beanpole.

'I have come to help you, Señor Shaw,' he said, and before John Gideon could object he continued, 'My *padre* – he wishes this. All my family are well – all my family wish this.'

The young Mexican stood with his hat in his hand, nervous excitement causing him to twist and turn it in the silence that followed. John Gideon shook his head. 'Where we are going Mano, it could be too dangerous for you. It's best for you to go home.'

Mano showed his disappointment.

'Wait,' Jack Hart said, 'we may be able to use him. Let's get to San Credo and see how the land lies.'

Mano looked to John Gideon.

'If Captain Hart says it's OK, you're in.'

Mano was overjoyed and joined the others at the table for a welcome meal.

San Credo lay about a full day's ride to the north-east of Acuna, and the strange assortment of riders, consisting of a lanky trail cook, a young Mexican boy, a fit, young ranger and his ageing, less able companion, left Acuna at a steady gait. Their journey was comfortable and uneventful and they stopped only once for a stretch, a cold snack and to water the horses.

They slowed down to a walk as they entered the environs of the town. San Credo was bigger and more sprawling than Acuna and they carefully steered their horses along the busy main street, as they scrutinized the establishments either side of the dirt road.

Jack Hart's bones ached as he got down from his mount at the first boarding-house they saw advertising clean rooms and good food.

'Here's a job for you, young Mano,' Captain Hart said. 'Go in and give the place the once over. Let's know if it's what it says it is.'

Mano sprang down eagerly from his horse

to obey the ranger captain.

Jack Hart grinned. 'You'd better go with him,' he said to John Gideon, who dismounted and passed his lead to his boss.

As they entered the door, the Mexican owner stepped into view. He studied Mano and the big ranger. Instantly dismissing the young Mexican, he bowed slightly to John Gideon.

'Good day, *señor.* You wish a room?' His English was good and he spoke precisely, wishing to impress the Americano.

Mano, not wishing to be ignored, asked the proprietor if the rooms were clean. The owner glowered at the young Mexican before he addressed John Gideon again.

'Room very clean. No bugs,' he beamed, adding, 'Food good. You like?'

The place and the owner certainly seemed cleaner than most places John Gideon had lodged in. Mano, not to be done out of his job, put on an air of seriousness and wandered through the downstairs rooms, inspecting as he went. John Gideon waited till Mano returned and gave his nod of approval before asking, 'Have you room for four of us?'

'*Si, señor.* Come, I show you.' The owner led them through the building. There were quite a few rooms available; most with one bed, some with two cots. Each room was clean, though Mano routinely inspected the beds and their covers, much to the chagrin of the Mexican owner.

'Anybody else staying here?' John Gideon asked, as they returned to the front desk.

'No. They go today,' the owner answered.

'OK, it will do. We'll take a double and two single rooms.'

Mano hastened to translate but the proprietor dismissed him with a wave of his hand.

'One two bed, two one bed, *señor,*' he confirmed with a smirk of satisfaction.

John Gideon nodded in agreement and went outside to tell Jack Hart and Buck Beanpole who had, in the meanwhile, lifted their saddles and warbags and were standing looking about, studying the people and busy life of San Credo.

Mano scooted past John Gideon and, loading himself up with warbags, he disappeared back into the boarding house.

'That young 'un's certainly eager to please,' Buck Beanpole commented, with a hint of disapproval.

'Don't worry about him, Buck, he does as he's told. Got good discipline for a youngster. He's just out to impress you at the moment. He'll settle down, you'll see,' John Gideon soothed.

The young ranger commandeered Mano to help him stable the horses, leaving Jack Hart and the lanky cook to sort out which room they were occupying. By the time the two got back to the boarding-house, Jack Hart had ordered a meal for them and the four sat down and ate heartily.

After the evening meal, the four travellers retired to their beds, with John Gideon and Mano sharing the double room. It had been a long ride from Acuna and they needed all the rest they could get for next day could prove to be a trying one.

Ned Embrel and his two henchmen, Crawford and Hall made their way to the town barber.

The sun beat down on the three men. From under his hat, Embrel's hair hung lank and greasy to his collar. He wiped his neck with his neckerchief.

'It's time we got cleaned up,' he said, rubbing his chin as he spoke.

'This heat is getting me down,' Crawford muttered. 'I think I'll get this stuff off, today.' His hair, too, straggled limply on his shoulders. Hall agreed.

The three raiders had talked over their next job. This time, Embrel had joked, they would ride out 'clean-shaved and handsome'.

The gang leader was beginning to get ready for the next meeting with his men. It was getting near to the time when Embrel's gang would ride out again. Wilson should be arriving soon – so should Jansen and his mob. This time, Embrel had said, they were going north – up to Kansas, then to Montana and maybe on into Canada. Hall had shuddered, thinking about the cold and snow of the north country.

Entering the barber's establishment, Embrel sat down in the chair. He watched critically as the barber removed his whiskers and trimmed his hair close.

Embrel's quips about getting a close shave amused his associates, but the barber had heard it all before and carried on till all three were 'tidied and presentable'.

Then the three raiders sampled the hot tub in the back, before donning their new change of clothes which they had had sent over from the store. They came from the bath house unrecognizable as the three who had entered an hour earlier. They still had money to spend and time to spend it in the forthcoming days.

A deep thirst and the gambling urge, beckoned them to the nearest saloon.

Two cowhands joined them in a game of poker and luck rode high in the strangers' favour, each taking over twenty dollars from the trio, in the early stages. Hall was in favour of taking the money back at gun-point, but Embrel, not wanting to draw attention to themselves at that time, disagreed, so things were left as they were and play continued.

It was at that stage of the game that John Gideon Shaw entered the saloon with Buck Beanpole and Jack Hart. It was the third saloon they had visited that day. Three beers were ordered and taken to a table at the back of the barroom from where they could study each individual table. They saw Embrel's table where five men played card. None of the card players looked like raiders – they looked clean-cut and seemed affably disposed by nature. From that table their glance swept across to others, then to the individuals standing at the bar. They could not decide who could be the guilty parties they were looking for.

Beanpole was getting short-tempered and impatient. He glanced belligerently at every customer.

'Perhaps the Mexican kid will have better luck than us,' he grumbled.

'Relax, Buck,' John Gideon told him. 'Enjoy your beer.' Buck snorted and took a deep draught.

Captain Hart's attention was drawn to the five card players again. One of the players slammed his cards down on the table, cursing his bad luck as the pot winner was picking up the money. The poor loser's hand was rubbing his outer thigh and his fingers hovered near his gun holster. Hart saw the man next to him lean across to whisper in his ear as he knocked his hand away. The game winner did not see the action of the two men as he busily stacked the coins, while talking excitedly to his companion, who smiled and nodded at what he heard. The ranger captain studied each individual at the table. It was obvious that two of them were having more luck with the cards than the rest.

Buck Beanpole fidgeted in his seat, his eyes roaming the barroom – searching for the man Embrel. What did he look like, this animal who had killed Nell? Hatred burned deep in the big man's heart as he thought about the gentle saloon girl he had learned to have more than a soft spot for. He looked across to John Gideon and, reading nothing in the young ranger's face he wondered what luck Mano, was having. Would he do better talking to the shop owners and other Mexican inhabitants of the town. Beanpole shook his head slowly – the Mexican kid could end up dead or give the game away and get them all caught unawares. He turned to complain to Jack Hart to find him frowning into his glass.

'What is it, Jack?' the lanky cook asked leaning towards the old ranger. Hart's manner gave nothing away. He picked up his glass, inspected its contents and sipped at his beer, before speaking.

'There are five card players over by the window. It looks like two of them are having more luck than the rest and the other three are not very pleased. The pots seem larger than usual and there seems to be some tension building.'

John Gideon tilted his head to take in the window area before commenting on his observation.

'They might be poor losers,' he proffered.

'Only certain poor losers contemplate shooting the winner,' Hart countered.

It was then that Hall scraped his chair away from the table as he slammed his cards down. 'I'm off to get myself a bit of fun. I've no luck here,' he complained, picking up his money.

The coins he stuffed agitatedly in his pants pocket before wrapping the few notes he still had round a roll he took from his shirt pocket. Replacing the wad of money carefully as he made his way across the doorway he paused to call back to his companions.

'Are you coming?' he shouted. 'Or d'you prefer their company to mine?' he added, glowering at the lucky poker winners.

'Wilson and the boys might come in,' Crawford said, in an attempt to keep the game running, 'What do you think, Ned?'

Embrel did not wish to discuss their intentions in public and could see that Hall was getting tetchy and argumentative. The gang leader began to pick up his money.

'It could be a few days yet before any of the boys ride in, and there's a couple of willin' doves I fancy soilin' just now, even if'n you don't,' Hall said loudly, getting more agitated and wanting to be off.

'OK, let's go,' Embrel said, straining a smile as he stood up and excused himself before pushing ahead of Crawford to join Hall, who by now was pacing the boardwalk outside.

'Perhaps your luck'll change, Hall. The way you're behaving, I reckon you could do with some,' Embrel gritted – the coldness in his voice registering his disapproval of Hall's outburst.

It was late afternoon as the three sauntered along the boardwalk before crossing over to visit their favourite whorehouse.

Inside the saloon, Captain Hart stopped Buck Beanpole from rising and following the three men.

'Not you Buck,' he said, before addressing the younger ranger. 'You go visit, John Gideon, and see if you can find out anything about them.'

The two lucky card players had by now risen from the table and, with their hands full of money, were approaching the bar.

As John Gideon left the saloon, Jack Hart grabbed Beanpole's arm, and raised his voice so it carried across to the bar. 'Reckon it's time to get us another drink, Buck, old-timer. It's my turn, I think. Sit tight. I'll be back in a flash.' As the cook stared at him in partial disbelief, the old ranger rose and made his way to the bar, to stand alongside the poker winners.

The barkeeper asked for their orders, waiting to see who spoke first.

'Go ahead, gentlemen, you first,' Jack Hart

said, rummaging about in his pocket, before swinging round to call to Beanpole, 'You want a whiskey. That right?'

'Have one on us, old-timer, and your friend,' the nearest cowhand offered, tossing some of the loose coins he had won on to the bar. 'Its our lucky day. They don't come any easier than them three as have just left. I hope their friends are just as easy when they arrive.'

'Why thanks,' Jack Hart said, ordering two whiskeys. 'I thought I'd seen them some-where before. Did any of them have a name?'

'They called one of them Ned. He seemed to be in charge,' the cowhand buying the drinks said, raising his glass and adding, 'Here's to Lady Luck.'

'May she stay awhile,' Hart replied, pick-ing up the two glasses and raising them in acknowledgement. Returning to his seat he sat down heavily with a sigh, 'From the young cowboy at the bar,' he said loudly, as he slid one of the drinks in front of

Beanpole. Turning towards the two at the bar, Buck raised his glass in salute before slugging the drink back in one gulp. The lucky cowboys nodded, drained their glasses and left the saloon to sample the food at the café the barkeep had recommended.

'Well?' The lanky cook raised his eyebrows, waiting for Jack Hart to say something.

'I think we're in luck,' the ranger said. 'One of the three goes by the name of Ned. He seems to be in charge and they're waiting for some others to ride in.'

'What do we do now?' Beanpole asked calmly. He knew it was up to Jack Hart to call the tune but whatever the orders, the lanky cook vowed silently that Ned Embrel – if he was one of the three – was his.

John Gideon kept a distance behind the three men. They went straight to their favourite house of ill-repute and entered. The young ranger strolled in shortly after them to witness a middle-aged madam welcoming Embrel and his two partners. She raised her eyebrows when she saw the tall handsome young stranger coming through the door and her smile widened, 'Ah, welcome, *señor*,' she beamed, turning back to Embrel. 'Are you all together?' It was Hall, still in a state of agitation, who turned to face the tall stranger, 'No we're not. And we get first choice of what's on offer.'

His look was challenging as he weighed up the tall, young man who returned the look with a calm unwavering glance, saying quietly, 'They were here first, ma'am. I can wait, and truth to tell I don't think me and the gent here would have the same taste in anything.'

Hall took the bait. 'Why you,' he countered, his hand dropping to his gun.

'Leave it,' Embrel barked out. 'We've come here for fun, not trouble. I'm sure there's plenty here for all of us.'

Embrel had quickly sized up the tall stranger – the cold eyes and the speed at which his hand had dropped to the Navy Colt at his hip. The .44 was halfway from its holster before Hall's hand had gripped the butt of his gun. Embrel knew this young man was not afraid to kill.

Hall snorted and took his hand away from his gun. The young ranger smiled coldly. 'As you say, sir, there's probably plenty for everyone. The name's Shaw.'

John Gideon ignored Hall as he introduced himself to Embrel, who was watching him like a cat watches a mouse.

'Name's Embrel, this here's Hall and Crawford.' He pointed to his two henchmen. 'I'm sure we can all be fixed up with the best of the madam's girls. She has always been satisfactory in the past.'

Embrel put his left hand on the shoulder of the slightly nervous brothel owner and gave her a pat and a slight shove. 'Let's see what you have.'

The woman hurried to the back, urgently calling the names of her girls. A young girl came through from the back, sleepy eyed and tousle-haired to be sent back with a scolding to go make herself presentable. The madam apologized profusely and disappeared to supervise the ablutions and presentation of her girls. The shouts and giggles as the women prepared themselves were all part of the show for the eager males.

'Shaw, did you say your name was? I don't reckon I've seen you around. Where are you from?' Embrel asked John Gideon.

'A lot of places,' the young ranger replied.

Ned Embrel nodded, knowing better than to push his questioning further.

The madam came in with one of her soiled doves. She wore a skimpy wrapper that covered very little and her tanned body glistened invitingly as she sashayed into the room. Hall stood up and threw his arm about her. 'This'll do me,' he said, glaring at John Gideon who did not respond but remained placid and seemingly unperturbed.

'Come on,' Hall said, as he mauled her, pulling her along to one of the rooms.

The young girl came through next with

one of the other women. She looked at John Gideon, her eyes warm and inviting. Embrel watched her, 'Go on, Shaw, the kid seems to have made the choice for you. Crawford can take the other one. I can wait.'

Crawford got up, keen to take the woman who was rounded and dimpled, just how he liked them. The tall ranger stood up and the young girl took his hand. The madam was smiling, pleased at their ready responses to her girls.

'Have it on me, Shaw,' Embrel said, reaching into his pocket. The madam's eyes gleamed at the roll of notes Embrel produced. It was not the first time the trio had visited her establishment and by the look of their bankroll she hoped it would not be the last. She recalled they spent well. This time they looked better dressed and more presentable than on previous visits but she never forgot a face if it belonged to a good spender.

'Here you are,' Embrel said, beckoning the madam over.

Crawford, Shaw and the two soiled doves left the room leaving the madam and Embrel alone. Embrel gave the woman the money and held her hand before taking an extra note and, waving it in front of her bosom, he muttered something in Spanish. She nodded as she snatched the money and quickly left the room.

Taking a towel and a bowl of water from the back room, she carried them to where the young girl was entertaining her tall, handsome client. Setting the bowl on the floor, the madam knocked at the door, opened it, picked up the bowl and bustled in.

The young girl had disrobed and looked surprised as her mistress entered.

'*Que pasa?*' she asked.

The madam smiled profusely at John Gideon who was freeing himself from the confines of his shirt.

'Water. The girl forgot the water, *señor.* She is young...'

She placed the bowl on the side table and

passed the towel to the girl speaking very quickly in her own tongue. John Gideon waited patiently, his fingers in his waistband, for the madam to finish what she was saying and leave. He did not understand what was being said but saw that the young girl was quite perturbed when her mistress left.

'Pardon, *señor.* I forget. I wash you now,' the young girl said, going to the side table and lifting the bowl of water.

'I can do that for myself. It's no problem,' John Gideon said softly, making to take the bowl from her.

'No. I get trouble ... big trouble,' she countered and pulled with greater force than was necessary to wrestle the bowl back from him.

The bowl went up in the air and the water splashed over the girl, the bed and the bedding.

'I get trouble. Big trouble for me,' the girl whimpered.

John Gideon handed her the towel. 'Here dry yourself. I'll go and explain to your boss. I'll be back soon,' he said, adding, 'with some water. *Aqua? Si?'*

'*Si, señor. Gracias,*' the girl said, wiping her face and hair as the tall young man disappeared through the door. The words of the madam rang in her ears. She quickly stepped over to the chair where his shirt had been discarded and her deft fingers searched the garment. She found loose money and his ranger's badge. Finding nothing else, she hurriedly replaced them and set about stripping the damp top cover from the bed. The thin mattress she tossed over and laid herself down to await the return of the handsome young man.

Running her fingers through her damp hair she wondered why madam had asked her to look through the young man's pockets to see if she could find out who he was. A handsome stranger with a badge. For telling her mistress this she would be given extra money.

TWELVE

John Gideon took what was offered from the young girl and the experience lasted a while longer than he had expected. The girl was well taught and he smiled to himself as he lay back watching her as she got off the bed and with effortless grace slid her robe over her slim shoulders. It would be easy to forget she was a brothel whore, he decided and began to realize something of what Buck Beanpole must be feeling about Nell, who had been murdered in the massacre at Leeward. The pretty girl smiled as she opened the door and lingered for a while before leaving the room.

The madam was waiting for her in the main room where Ned Embrel waited to hear what the girl had to say. The young whore told the madam what she had found out and she in turn passed the information on. At the mention of the ranger badge, Embrel got to his feet and abruptly left the whorehouse. He hurried back to his lodging and collected his gear, which was already packed. His face was set and thunderous as he made his way to the town livery. Questions buzzed through his head, spawning more irritating thoughts. Was the young Texas Ranger on his trail? How did he find out who he was? And who were the two older men he had noticed with Shaw, in the saloon earlier? Were they setting a trap? Ned Embrel paid his dues and began to saddle up.

Where was Wilson and his lot? And Jansen? Some of his boys should have showed up by now. He halted the thought right there. Something, sure as hell, was wrong and he did not intend to hang around and find out what it was. The sooner he shook the dust of San Credo off his feet, the better.

With a final check to his gear, Embrel

swung into the saddle and, tugging at the reins, urged his horse through the stable doors and onto the main street. As he did so, a young Mexican darted across the road in front of him, causing his horse to stumble and rear. Embrel cursed the falling Mexican as he fought to keep control of his animal. The horse regained its footing and galloped off down the main street.

The fallen youth, dazed by the experience, sat in the road, watching the horse and rider leave San Credo in a cloud of swirling dust. Then, getting to his feet, he fingered his cheekbone tentatively and winced. Mano checked the rest of his body and finding himself still in one piece went to the nearest saloon, where he found Beanpole and the ranger captain sitting at a table. There was no sign of John Gideon Shaw.

'Ah, young Mano,' Jack Hart declared, signalling for the boy to join them.

'Did you find out anything?' Mano shook his head.

'What happened to you?' Buck Beanpole

asked him, taking a piece of cloth from his pocket.

'I was run down by a gringo leaving San Credo in a hurry. But I am OK, *señor*. It is only a scratch.' The young Mexican took the proffered cloth and dabbed at his cheek.

Jack Hart stood up. Before he could speak, gunfire rang out somewhere down the street.

'Come on,' he said and, with Beanpole masking Mano behind him, the threesome went outside.

A woman's screaming directed their attention along the road apiece to the entrance of one of the town's establishments, where two partly-clad women were standing, one comforting the other, whose skimpy covering was splattered in blood. Captain Jack Hart pulled his .45 and hurried down the street.

Minutes earlier the scene had been totally different.

Inside the whorehouse, John Gideon Shaw had washed and towelled and started dressing.

The last thing he did was put on his gun-belt. Automatically, he pulled his Navy Colt, checked it and replaced it. The door opened and, much to John Gideon's surprise, the pretty young whore re-entered.

'Well, hello again,' he mused, 'but I really must get going.'

She smiled, broadly. 'You very 'andsome, *señor.*' The girl struggled to speak in English.

'So are you. *Bella, mucha bella,*' the ranger said, bending to kiss her cheek.

The girl stared at him, then her face clouded over.

'What is it? *Que pasa?*' he asked. She grabbed his arm, her fingers gripping tightly in an attempt to hold him back as he made to leave. John Gideon gently but firmly re-moved her hand. He could hear the men's coarse voices as they shouted to each other. He had to report to Jack Hart while Embrel and his men were still here, in the whore-house.

'No, *señor,*' the girl tried once more to stop John Gideon.

207

'What's wrong? *Que pasa?*' he repeated, frustration at their poor communication, making his voice brittle and uncompromising. Shaw could have done with an interpreter and wished Mano or Jack Hart were close by. The young whore clutched at his pocket, where she knew his badge lay.

'Ranger,' she drawled, remembering Embrel's use of the word when she had told her mistress about the badge. It began to dawn on John Gideon that something had happened. He took his badge out of his pocket and thrust it towards her.

'Who knows?' he asked.

The girl began to cry and placed herself with her back to the door. John Gideon pushed her to one side and went out to confront the owner. The young girl let out a wail of anguish.

'What is happening?' the madam asked, jumping up from her seat at the sight of the angry young man.

Crawford came from his room. He was carrying his gun-belt and the woman he had been with was close behind him.

'What the hell's going on here? Who are you, mister, and what's your beef?' He focused on the tall stranger and spotted the star in Shaw's hand.

'Where's Embrel?' he demanded, his voice rising in alarm as he tried to pull his gun from his holster. 'Hall, get out here,' he shouted.

John Gideon reacted. His hand came up with a blur. His gun exploded as Crawford's gun came level. The bullet from Shaw's Navy Colt hit Crawford in the chest. Then again the ranger fired as he fanned the hammer. The second slug hit Crawford in the head and he fell against the Mexican whore, trapping her against the door frame. His gun dropped from his hand and blood poured from his head and chest as he slid down the woman. She tried to pull away in horror, but Crawford's fingers clutched at her flimsy housecoat as he fell to the floor.

Hall came from his room, his Colt in one hand and the woman with whom he had been laughing and joking until a few moments ago, in the other. She whimpered in abject fear as Hall positioned her in front of him, and froze as the gun alongside her body exploded. The raider had fired at John Gideon but the shot went wild as Hall caught sight of Crawford sprawled on the floor.

John Gideon Shaw returned the fire. The .44 slug hit Hall in the face, that being the only part exposed above the cringing woman. He fell backwards, his second shot exploding into the ceiling. The terrified whore broke free, screaming, to join her friend and both ran out of the premises hoping, by doing so, to escape the carnage.

The madam cursed as the older whores scurried past her. What if they ran off back to their village? And who would pay for the ceiling and to clean up the place and to bury the dead? And what about her good name? Composing herself, the madam grabbed the young girl, still whimpering by the wrist.

'*Señor.* What about the damage. Who will

pay for–' Her tirade was cut short as the young ranger's gun swung round to nestle purposefully close to her heart.

'Where's the other one, Madam?' Shaw demanded. The young girl blessed herself with her free hand. The brothel owner saw the cold eyes of the young ranger and knew he meant business.

'Gone,' she said.

Suddenly the door was pushed wide open and Jack Hart entered, his Colt .45 in his fist.

Buck Beanpole and Mano were close behind. The ranger captain's sweeping gaze took in the scene and the two corpses.

'Where's the third one?' he asked John Gideon.

'Gone, according to her,' the ranger said, nodding towards the madam.

Buck Beanpole cursed out loud and dragged the wide-eyed, slack-mouthed young Mano outside away from the scene of death and scantily clad women.

'She used the girl to search my clothes and

found my badge,' John Gideon continued. 'She told Embrel and it looks like he hightailed it, leaving those two behind.'

Captain Hart glanced at the madam whose blustering had given way to silence at the sight of the armed rangers. 'He paid well,' she said, excusing her behaviour.

The two older whores backed in through the door as a group of townsfolk gathered and crowded round the establishment, looking in through the doorway and curtained windows. The madam sighed with relief to find her girls had not deserted her and directed them to take themselves and the young girl into the back room. With a degree of composure, she turned to face the rangers.

'Get them buried,' Hart barked before she could launch forth again. Shaw had searched the dead raiders' bodies and found their stashes of money.

'There's more than enough there,' he said, throwing some notes contemptuously onto the bodies. 'Come on, let's go and find

Embrel. We know what he looks like now.'

They left the brothel and pushed their way through the straggle of spectators to find Beanpole and Mano waiting for them.

'Señor Shaw, Señor Shaw. I am so happy you are OK,' the Mexican boy shrilled, as he quick-stepped alongside John Gideon.

Shaw noticed the graze on his young friend's face and pulling up short, he swung the youth round in front of him. 'How come you're not so okay? What happened?' he asked.

'A gringo rode me down,' Mano replied simply.

Captain Jack Hart cursed out loud, as the truth dawned on him. 'According to Mano the gringo rode out in a hurry. You can bet it was Embrel. Best get after him.'

The four hurried to the town stables.

Jack Hart led the way out of San Credo, following the direction Ned Embrel had taken.

Outside the town, the ranger captain reined in and looked to the back trail which led to Acuna. Jack Hart cursed softly under his breath as he realized there was no way he could pick out the trail Embrel had taken. Had the gang leader gone to Acuna, hoping to meet up with Wilson and his gang or would he have gone to the American States to disappear for a while before regrouping with a new gang? The old ranger decided that Embrel would go to the nearest Mexican town – which in this case was Acuna – hoping to find some of his men. He would be on his guard, knowing at least one ranger was on his trail and as such could be dangerous if cornered. In their favour – of the four of them – Mano was a wild card. Jack Hart did not think Embrel was aware of the young Mexican's existence. And the gang leader was not yet aware that all of his gang had been wiped out.

Riding with speed and skill, Ned Embrel swore to himself as he thought back on the series of events that had driven him from San Credo. The appearance of the ranger in the brothel had come as a complete surprise. It shouldn't have. He chided himself for his laxity. For a man who was always aware of personal danger, in the evil way of life he had chosen, warning bells should have rung out when he saw the quick reaction of the young stranger to Hall's threat.

Embrel had never seen anybody quicker – not even Wilson. And Wilson? Where the hell was he? He should, by now, be heading this way towards San Credo.

The day had not gone well, starting with the greenhorn cowboys beating them at poker. He should have let Hall drive the two tinhorns out of town. Embrel grunted and dug his heels into his horse's flanks. He sensed Hall and Crawford would be lucky to get away uninjured from the whorehouse in San Credo. Hall would find out how fast the young stranger was with his gun. His temper could be his downfall. Still, Hall's confrontation with the ranger, would give Embrel the time he needed to put distance between himself and San Credo.

Even leaving the town had not been incident free. He should have mown down that Mexican kid. It would have been good gun practice. Embrel began to regain his animal sense for survival. He was good with a gun – even if he did prefer shooting a man from behind – and he had a good nose for a hold-up. Men and horses were never a problem as those who threatened to become one were quickly disposed of. In fact, that was his philosophy, if he really thought about it. Everything, including man and beast, was disposable. Things needed to get back to the way they were.

He scanned the road ahead. Where the hell was Wilson?

Jack Hart made his decision and the foursome took the road back to Acuna.

It was impossible to read sign on the well-trodden trail, but instinct told the ranger captain that Embrel would be heading that way hoping to meet some of his gang members making their way to San Credo and thinking there would be safety in numbers. The old ranger rode steadily in front with the lanky cook for company. John Gideon Shaw kept his grulla at a steady gait with Mano following in his wake.

The town of Acuna was lit up by the time Embrel arrived. He had left his mount, tethered and hobbled, outside of town at a spot that had water and grass in a cluster of trees. Then, with his saddle-bag containing his money slung over his shoulder, he trudged into town. Glancing often at his back trail, he was comforted to find there was no sign of any followers. Perhaps Hall and Crawford between them had taken care of the ranger and his companions.

Embrel's spirits rose and he soon found a place to stay before walking to the town stables to look for the mounts of Wilson and his crew. He was lucky and found them.

He asked the stable owner if the riders had been in lately. The Mexican shrugged, saying nothing, showing no awareness of what the gringo wanted to know.

Unbeknown to Embrel, the stable owner had purchased the horses, paying the town's undertaker enough money to bury the four previous owners. As a matter of fact, he had five good horses, with Bradshaw's mount.

Embrel told the Mexican that if the owners came in later to tell them that Ned Embrel was in town, looking them up. He paid the ostler a dollar for his trouble and left. The dollar was pocketed. The Mexican smiled to himself. Gringos, he thought, too much money.

Embrel entered the first saloon he came to and scanned the room but could not see any of his gang members. He searched on. It was at one of the bars that he asked after Wilson and a cowboy, who was drinking at the bar, overheard him enquiring.

'Was he handy with a gun? A runt of a fella?' he asked Embrel.

Embrel looked the man over. Was he another of the rangers?'

'Could be. Do you know where he is?'

Embrel's hand lowered, by his gun.

'Yes, I know where he is. He's in Boot Hill with the rest of his party.'

Embrel's jaw dropped. He could not believe what he was hearing.

'Who put him there?' Embrel inquired.

'Never had a name... Young fella ... tall... Word around town has it that he killed three of 'em and then rode out. There was five dead altogether that day, if my mem'ry serves me right.'

Ned Embrel left the saloon. He knew who the tall man was. It could only be Shaw.

He turned, headed for his lodgings, picked up his gear and walked to the livery. He needed to have a talk with the stable owner. He had a score to settle with him.

The Mexican heard the old door creak open and got up off his chair and went to see who had come into his stable. He came face to face with the gringo who, a while earlier, had paid him a dollar. The gringo stacked his gear against the nearest stall.

'Ah, *señor*, I can help you? *Si?*'

Ned Embrel straightened up, drew his gun and shot the ostler in the gut. The Mexican sank to his knees, his hands trying to stop the red liquid that was spurting from his body, pouring his life away. He felt the hands of the gringo go into his pocket and take the few dollars he found there. His vision blurred, but he heard the slight rustle as Ned Embrel shuffled about the stables.

The Mexican's last thought was a confusion about money and gringos.

Ned Embrel was alone. He dimmed the lights and carefully bar-locked the stable doors. Then, hefting his gear, he went into the back room and closed the door, extinguishing all but a meagre candlelight. Finding the coffee pot on the stove, he poured himself a cupful and sat on the newly vacated chair. He would ride out after his drink – away from Mexico – and head north up to Montana ... as far away from here and Texas as possible. He checked the money in his saddle-bag. It would keep him comfortable and undercover, if necessary, for a good while yet.

The sound of somebody trying the stable door broke into his thoughts.

A voice called out, 'Ostler are you in there?'

Embrel sat still and quiet. Putting the coffee down, he drew his gun.

'There's nobody in there. 'Come on,' the voice said. Embrel heard the sound of horses and then hurrying footsteps as they moved away. He replaced his gun.

At the corral tie rail, alongside the stable, the three men and the boy temporarily tethered their horses.

'That's unusual,' Jack Hart said. 'It's not like a livery to be all locked up.' Beanpole agreed.

'Perhaps the owner has gone to get something,' Mano said. 'I stay here with the horses, if you say. Till he gets back.' The young Mexican looked at the others eagerly, waiting for instructions. He was only too pleased to do something for his ranger friend.

'The kid's right. He could stay here while we search for Embrel,' Buck Beanpole said, keen to get searching for the gang leader. 'When that coyote finds Wilson ain't here, he's gonna hightail it quicker than a lightnin' flash.'

John Gideon agreed with Beanpole knowing he would be much happier if Mano stayed put. Embrel would shoot on sight if he saw any of them and the young Mexican would be safer at the stable, being unknown to the killer, Embrel.'

'That's settled then. You stay here, Mano,' the ranger captain instructed. 'If the owner gets back before we do, go inside and stay with him, do you understand?' Mano nodded as he watched the three men walk away to search for the *bandido* who had ridden him down in San Credo.

After a while the young Mexican got restless. He looked about. The mounts stood hip-shot after their journey from San Credo. Mano left them and moved closer to the locked door. He suddenly stopped still. He had heard something from inside the stables, it was the rasping of wood and metal. Mano stepped back quickly into the shadow of the building. Slowly the door opened and a man with a gun in his hand, and a saddle-bag over his shoulder, came from inside and looked about cautiously. Mano pressed himself further into the shadows and froze. The man looked over to where he stood but was distracted by the four mounts at the corral rail as they side-stepped and snickered. The man with the gun looked further afield for the owners but saw none. In the half-light Mano thought he recognized the man as the rider who had ridden him down in San Credo. He peered closer in the evening light, trying to see his face more clearly. As Mano moved he dislodged a discarded rake with his foot and it slid down the wall of the wooden building. Embrel's keen ears heard the sound and he responded by firing his gun into the shadows. A voice echoed out in pain. Embrel had scored a hit. The gang leader took to his heels and ran off, dodging into the shadows, eager to get away from the stable area, and made for the place where he had hobbled his mount.

Mano staggered back as he saw Embrel aim and fire. The bullet had sliced into the building, sending slivers of wood into his already grazed face. He cried out in pain and clutched at the damage. Then he heard the man take to his heels. Mano regained his balance in time to see the dark shape disappearing into the heavy gloom as night began to settle on the town.

His face throbbing, Mano entered the livery through the open door and, locating a water trough inside the stables, he sloshed his face with the cooling liquid. His eyes cleared and as he stood up to take stock of the building, a big hand gripped his shoulder.

'It's OK, Mano, it's me, Beanpole,' the lanky cook said, before loosening his grip to strike a match.

The young Mexican let out a gasp and

pointed to where on the floor close by, lay the body of the stable owner. Even from where they stood, Mano and Beanpole could see he was dead.

'There's nothing we can do for him,' the lanky cook concluded. 'But what's happened to you, boy? I heard shooting and came running. Did you see who took a shot at you?'

Buck Beanpole had by this time lit a lamp, sat Mano down and had bathed and inspected the damage. The boy's face was swollen and bloody and splinters of wood needed removing.

The lanky cook stood up, stretched and sighed. The bleeding had stopped. It would do for now.

'He look like the gringo who rode me down in San Credo. I think it was him, Señor Buck. He was here … in the stable … all the time. I think he did that one…' he said, pointing to the corpse, before adding, as if a light had been switched on, 'I see where he go.' The young Mexican ran outside the stable and pointed. 'He went that way.'

Buck Beanpole was galvanized into action. As he ran to his horse, he shouted to Mano to go find John Gideon and Jack Hart and tell them to follow on. Climbing aboard, he rode off into the night, hoping it was the right way and he was on the killer's trail. It might not be Embrel but whoever it was, he was a killer.

THIRTEEN

Mano had indicated that the gunman had hurried away from the stabling area which suggested he had his horse hidden somewhere, probably on the edge of town. His horse surged and two-stepped for a spell as Beanpole slapped and reined, his keen eyes raking the alleys as he left town. Once clear of the town's limits, Buck urged his mount forward, hoping it would not snag a hoof in the dark. He spotted a shadowy figure running towards a copse of trees.

Ned Embrel heard the hooves pounding behind him and turned to find a horse and rider powering recklessly towards him. He fired his .45 but the animal seemed unstoppable.

Embrel dropped his saddle-bags and, with both hands steadying his Colt, he fired again. The horse faltered. He fired once more at the falling animal before grabbing his saddle-bags and turning at an angle to flee. The trees ahead of him got nearer. If only he could reach cover and his horse. Footsteps pounded behind him. He turned in dismay to find a giant of a man closing in. He fired again but his gun clicked on an empty chamber. Then the big, long frame of Buck Beanpole was upon him. Cursing, Embrel swung first the handgun, then the saddle-bags at the man but it did not stop the big ranch cook's onslaught. The killer struggled to escape the giant's bear-hug as he felt the breath being squeezed out of him. The fingers of Buck Beanpole's big hands crawled to the throbbing neck of the gang leader who began to choke. Just before he blacked out the pressure was released and he found himself being held by his shirt front, with one hand, like a bundle of rags. He felt himself being pivoted on to his toes before a big fist was smashed into his face. Again and again it relentlessly pounded home. Then darkness took the pain away.

John Gideon walked from the saloon and looked across the street as Jack Hart came out of the building opposite him. He raised his hand in salute and shook his head, acknowledging the fact that Embrel was not hiding there either. His glance zigzagged back along the street for Beanpole, who had fallen behind the other two, as he double-checked each establishment.

Darting from the boardwalk onto the dirt road was a young boy. It was Mano, breathlessly shouting and waving, coming towards them.

'Will that young 'un never learn to look where he's going? He'll get himself run down for sure,' the ranger captain gritted, as he joined John Gideon.

The rangers hurried back towards the Mexican boy and John Gideon urged the lad to take a deep breath so they could make sense of his garbled outburst.

'Señor Shaw,' the lad gasped pointedly.

'That's better, Mano, now keep it about that pace.'

They listened with heads bowed as the young Mexican recounted slowly and deliberately what had happened.

Arriving back at the stables, the rangers told Mano to untie their horses from the corral rail, and wait there till they got back. They reconnoitred the immediate area around the livery barn before venturing inside. The ostler lay where Mano had told them and it did not need a doctor to tell them he was dead. A quick inspection of the stables told them nothing further so the rangers, seeing nothing could be done for the owner, went back outside, and climbed aboard their horses to go in pursuit of Embrel and Buck Beanpole.

They delayed only long enough to instruct Mano to ride well back, deciding it was better to take the young Mexican with them than to risk leaving him in town on his own. As they turned their horses out of town, they heard the dull bark of shots echoing through the night. They followed the sounds into the darkness, eyes and ears pricked sharp and nerves taut as guitar strings. Their path led them towards a shadowy stretch of wooded area which they approached with caution.

As they neared the copse, they came across the bulky carcass of Beanpole's fallen mount but there was no sign of the lanky cook. They dismounted and, leading their horses, they slowly entered the trees.

In the meantime, Buck Beanpole had dragged the unconscious Embrel further into the trees. In so doing, he came across the raider's saddled horse from which he procured a rope and a water bottle before dragging Embrel further into the trees. Reaching a spot that satisfied him, Buck Beanpole allowed Embrel to slump to the ground. Unscrewing the water bottle he trickled the contents over Embrel's head. Slowly the outlaw killer began to come to his senses. He could smell blood and damp earth and he muttered something through swollen lips as he struggled to get to a sitting position. It was then that he made out the tall gangling figure of his attacker.

'Who are you?' he managed to gasp.

Buck Beanpole did not answer him. He was looking about him. Finding what he needed, he tossed the rope over the stoutest limb of the tree he had chosen. Then he came and stood over Embrel. Without a word, Beanpole stooped down and dragged the gang leader, like a sack of flour, to the appointed tree, where he placed the noose of the rope over Embrel's head. It was about then that urgent signals began to fight their way through to Embrel's brain and he realized what his lanky captor was going to do.

He started to struggle, kicking out at the big man who was pulling him roughly to his feet. Buck Beanpole deftly side-stepped before tightening the rope. Ned Embrel was pulled abruptly upright to stand on his tiptoes. His hands tugged at the rope around his neck as he half-pirouetted round to look into the face of the tall man. Embrel could almost feel the flames of hatred in the lanky giant's eyes. As his feet left the ground, the killer's tongue began to swell and fill his mouth. His feet kicked about wildly, trying to find some purchase. Then he was pulled higher as Buck Beanpole heaved on the rope. The night turned red and purple, then black for Ned Embrel as he got what his exploits had earned him – death by hanging.

Buck Beanpole stood still, his muscles bunched and his arms aching, as the lifeless body swung to and fro on the rope.

It was at that precise moment that Jack Hart, leading the trio, saw the swinging body. He signalled a halt and stepped back to whisper to John Gideon to stay put and keep the boy with him. Ground hitching his horse, he moved stealthily forward. As he parted the undergrowth, the scene unfolded before him and he could make out the tall figure of Buck Beanpole as the lanky cook released the rope and let the body fall to the ground. He hollered ahead and started forward again. Buck Beanpole recognized the old ranger's voice and turned to see Jack Hart coming towards him.

'You're too late, Jack. I've given him his comeuppance.

Joining the ranch cook, the ranger captain stooped to examine the inert body at his feet. He felt for any sign of life but there was none. He struck a match and saw the facial damage that had been inflicted on the outlaw killer, which he knew was the work of the big man alongside of him. Buck Beanpole had finally avenged the tragic death of his woman, Nell. The right or wrong of his action was blown away as Jack Hart extinguished the flickering match.

Together they dragged the corpse of the dead gang leader into the bushes and covered it with debris before walking away without a second glance. Neither man spoke as Buck Beanpole led the way to where Ned Embrel's horse had been left. Jack Hart watched as the lanky cook freed the horse and stood for a while, his face buried in the horse's neck.

'His saddle-bags are at the edge of the copse,' Beanpole announced gruffly as he swung into the saddle.

John Gideon and Mano heard Jack Hart's voice before they spotted him leading Ned Embrel's horse towards them with Buck Beanpole in the saddle.

'That's another job finished,' the ranger captain announced as he mounted up, adding, 'I'll put all the details in my report when we get back to Austin.'

John Gideon knew it was Jack Hart's way of warning him not to question him further at that moment.

'Is the *bandido* dead, Señor Shaw?' the young Mexican whispered, leaning over towards his companion as they made their way out of the copse.

'I guess so,' John Gideon answered. Mano waited expectantly for more details but none were forthcoming.

The foursome halted on the edge of the copse while Beanpole and the captain dismounted to search for the saddle-bags. Retrieving them, Jack Hart managed a grin as he mounted his horse and hauled alongside Mano.

'It's about time we got you home, young fella. Your pa will be mighty proud to hear how you helped us catch up with the *bandidos*, though what your mama will say when she sees your face, is something else altogether,' Jack Hart said, drawing attention to the weals and deep scratches left by the splinters and the skinning the young Mexican had suffered.

'To be a man, I must be brave. This my *padre* say to me,' Mano stated proudly, fingering his scarred cheek. 'My *madre* will cry but she will know I am a man.'

Buck Beanpole, aboard Ned Embrel's horse, lined up behind the other three.

'OK, young man, I reckon it's your turn to take the lead. Show us where you live,' Jack Hart said. Mano clicked his horse ahead and set off at a fair pace. Perhaps there would be a reward! The young Mexican's heart was singing as he imagined the reunion with his family.

Did he have a tale to tell!

The publishers hope that this book has given you enjoyable reading. Large Print Books are especially designed to be as easy to see and hold as possible. If you wish a complete list of our books please ask at your local library or write directly to:

Dales Large Print Books
Magna House, Long Preston,
Skipton, North Yorkshire.
BD23 4ND